THE BILLIONAIRE
SMOKEJUMPER

ESCAPE TO SUN VALLEY

SARAH GAY

\

LITERARY EVOLUTION

ALSO BY SARAH GAY

All books in the

Grant Brothers Billionaire Boss Romance

Series:

Her Reluctant Boss: Book 1

sarahgay.com/her-reluctant-boss

The Billionaire Patriot: Book 2

sarahgay.com/the-billionaire-patriot

The Billionaire Smokejumper: Book 3

sarahgay.com/the-billionaire-smokejumper

The Billionaire Champion: Book 4

sarahgay.com/the-billionaire-champion

The Billionaire Hockey Star: Book 5

sarahgay.com/the-billionaire-hockey-star

Once Upon a Midnight Kiss: Book 6

sarahgay.com/once-upon-a-midnight-kiss

The Billionaire Fake Fiancé: Book 7

sarahgay.com/the-billionaire-fake-fiance

The Last Billionaire: Book 8

sarahgay.com/the-last-billionaire

NEWSLETTER—FREE BOOK, GIVEAWAY, AND SPECIAL OFFERS

To receive a free copy of Sarah Gay's best-selling book, Her Guardian Boss Fake Fiancé, simply join her mailing list on her website SarahGay.com.

By signing up, you'll get a first look at new releases, special offers, and learn how to register for giveaways.

Enjoy your FREE book today!

CHAPTER ONE

*O*nce upon a time, there was a little girl in rural Idaho. On cold days, when she didn't dare leave her house for fear of freezing to death, she stared out her frosted window and dreamt of sunny beaches and a handsome boy to fetch her cotton candy and corn dogs.

The girl grew...

"Mariah?" Sebastian's voice pulled her into the present.

"Huh?" With her cell phone pressed to her ear, she cast her eyes around her cream-colored cubicle, trying to remember why he'd called.

Sebastian humphed his annoyance into the phone. "So... do you want to go with me this weekend for your birthday? You've been talking about your ten-year anniversary all year."

My birthday! Birthdays still gave her the magical feeling of Christmas morning. A decade earlier, when she'd turned eighteen, she'd decided it was time to live her dream. People called her a math whiz. Numbers had always been her thing. That day, eighteen became her new lucky number. She'd loaded her car with nonessentials, kissed her parents goodbye, and set the timer on her watch for eighteen hours. With happy flutters of adventure in her stomach, she drove in search of sunshine and surf. When her alarm sounded eighteen hours later, she stared out her window at Sacramento, California. Her first stop was a mom-and-pop diner off I-80. The owners offered her a job on the spot. It didn't take long to fall in love with the city. Beautiful trees, lively city life, and perfect weather. Home.

"Mariah?"

She blinked. "To the beach?" she said with excitement. "You know I'm always game. We could hit Muir beach, then head up to Bodega Bay. Or stick with my happy place, Santa Cruz. When I moved to Sacramento, I had no idea there would be so many beach options within less than three-hours' drive."

Life was just how she'd planned it. She stared at the photo of the Santa Cruz boardwalk tacked to her cubicle. In the photo, she bit into a corn dog from Surf City Grill while Sebastian laughed at her for wanting to take a selfie of biting into a corn dog. Simple minds couldn't comprehend the pure joy of a perfectly fried corn dog while breathing in the salty sea air.

"No," Sebastian said with a sigh. "Not the beach. I asked you if you want to go to Idaho with me this weekend."

She scratched above her ear. "Sorry. I'm confused. Why do you want to vacation in Idaho again?"

The office door opened. A spine-chilling breeze blasted through the room. Fear gripped Mariah's chest, causing Sebastian's voice to fade. She set her phone onto her desk. Frozen in place, she didn't look up as the dark shadow approached from behind.

Audible shivers cascaded down the sixteen occupied cubicles, skipping over the thirty-two vacant ones. When the HR director came into the room, everyone in Mariah's department held their breath. September had been a month of record layoffs due to recent restrictions on elective surgeries. October was proving similarly devastating. Less medical claims meant less need for claims officers to process them.

The tall apparition lurked behind her chair. She bit her lower lip as a flat mailing envelope slid across her desk. The rough paper scraped against the wood veneer, making the sound of an ocean wave as it stripped the shore on its way back out to sea.

"Sorry about this, Mariah," came the HR director's legitimately apologetic voice. She held back her tears and simply nodded. He cleared his throat. "In this folder, you'll find three letters of recommendation and two months' severance." He placed his hand on her shoulder. "Good luck." He left the room as swiftly as he'd come.

She had no job, or any hope of one; employment wasn't easy to come by. At least she still had a boyfriend. She placed the phone to her ear. "Idaho sounds lovely."

～

*S*eventy-two hours later, Mariah Larkin pedaled her rented mountain bike with increased zeal. The bike trail stretched on for miles as it wound along the trickling river. The afternoon sunshine warmed her shoulders while happy endorphins tickled her brain, causing a smile to spread across her face. Her first real smile in days.

The mid-October breeze blew into the tips of the tall trees that lined the bike path, causing the tree limbs to crackle. Red and yellow leaves released from their branches, slowly flittering to the damp earth.

Mariah skidded to an abrupt stop. "I never knew Idaho

could be so beautiful," she said with a long sigh as colorful leaves swept the pebbled path in front of her.

Sebastian braked at her side. "Please don't tell me you want to move back anytime soon."

With a coy smile, she let him know she knew he was teasing her. "You're the one who brought me here. I finally understand why you Californians vacation in Sun Valley. The fall colors are to die for." She stretched her arms up at her sides. "And just look at all this open space, fresh air, and untamed mountain peaks."

"It's great, but *untamed* isn't the word I'd use," he said, motioning to Bald and Dollar mountain ranges. Ski runs chunked out sections of trees on the mountains' rounded peaks, like wide rivers of lava flowing down a volcano.

She tsked her tongue. "I was talking about those." She pointed to the east toward Pioneer mountain range, then to the north to the Boulder Mountains. "Untamed mountains roll on for miles and miles and miles. We don't have mountains like these where I grew up. All we had was ice and cold."

Idaho's only redemptive quality was the kind and loving people it produced. Until this trip, that's what she'd always thought. She'd never known anyone to vacation in *her* rural town, eight hours north of there. She didn't blame vacationers for not coming; after living in California, even she, an Idaho native, had sworn off living in Idaho due to the state's harsh winters.

But before winter, came the change of seasons—and Sun Valley changed seasons with flare, fire-and-ice style. Earlier that morning, fresh snowfall had blanketed the trees' high branches and frost had carpeted the forest floor. Nothing compared to the contrast between changing leaves and brilliant white snow.

Sebastian rode his bike in a circle around her. "We can't

stop every five minutes, or this ride will take all day and we'll miss our dinner at the Mandolin. I made reservations six months ago when the Mandolin received three Michelin stars and was touted the best French restaurant in the west."

She'd never quite understood Sebastian's obsession with French cuisine. A salmon-colored leaf settled onto her shoulder. "I'm turning over a new leaf," she chuckled to herself, holding the leaf out in front of her face. "No better time to start my New Year's resolutions than now."

"Works for me. I have next week off. Let's drive toward the Grand Canyon tomorrow instead of home. We could hike rim to rim on Monday."

She shot him a disapproving glare. "You say that like twenty-five miles of strenuous mountain hiking is a piece of cake."

"It's closer to twenty-three miles. And it's not *too* difficult," he said, casting his eyes up at Dollar Mountain, its rounded tips sprinkled with fresh snow.

Mariah clicked her tongue at him.

He stared at her with an egotistical expression. "I know what I'm talking about. I hiked the Grand with my frat brothers. All you need are some new hiking shoes. It's about a fourteen-hour drive from here. With meal stops, we can make it there in around eighteen hours."

"Did you say eighteen hours?" She wrinkled her nose in thought. Perhaps he *did* know what they'd be getting themselves into, but she had to be sure. "Don't people normally train for like a year or two before they hike the Grand Canyon?"

He released a deep chortle. "I didn't train at all the last time, and I was just fine."

Her sense of adventure peaked. "You really think I could hike it without any training?"

"Absolutely. And you're the one who said you wanted to

lose some weight." He gave her a once over. "If you don't put in the effort, the only thing you'll lose is time."

Sensitivity and patience weren't Sebastian's strong points, but he was handsome, so she cut him slack…way too often. With his thick wavy curls, boyish face, and huge brown eyes, he didn't look a day over twenty-one—which wasn't necessarily a good thing. When they'd started casually dating last year, they'd matched up well. She'd felt like his equal back then. Sitting for ten hours a day had caused her body to get squishy and lumpy. Not to mention, she looked her age.

Mariah stepped off her bike to examine her thick thighs and pudgy muffin top. Whoever invented skintight biking attire for novices, they needed to retire, like yesterday. She walked over to the trickling brook at the edge of the path and stared down at the water as it bubbled over multicolored rocks, contemplating her options. If she kick-started her exercise routine with a strenuous hike, like the Grand Canyon, it would get her motivated to keep it up. Climbing out of bed the past two mornings had been tough enough. Depression had caught hold of her like nothing she'd ever experienced before.

When she'd called her parents to tell them she'd been let go, her dad had told her that no matter how bad she felt, she needed to eat healthy, exercise, and get plenty of sunshine. In theory, his suggestions were spot on. The first two days after her layoff, she'd followed his advice, but it hadn't helped her feel any better.

Today was a different story. The Idaho sunshine, fresh air, and exercise was exactly what she needed to snap out of her funk. Inspiration tickled her mind. She'd neglected her body's needs for far too long. It craved physical care. She had *one* body. It was finally time to start listening to her old bag of bones.

Body reformation! She would start strong. No holding

back. The concept of hitting it hard from the get-go agreed with her psyche. Every year, she set her New Year's resolutions in mid-October, instead of the first of January. She liked the idea of getting a head start on her goals. She twisted her lips in thought. She'd planned to do early morning cardio at the gym and late evening swims at the swim and tennis club, but she could no longer afford those memberships. Hiking the Grand Canyon would be an excellent way to kick-start her body reformation routine.

"Let's do it!" she said with renewed purpose. She waved for Sebastian to follow her, straddled her bike, and sped down the path.

An hour later, they rode into downtown Ketchum. Brick buildings lined the wide, empty streets, lending the city an old town feel. She lazily zig-zagged down the street, imagining horse and carriage buggies clomping by. She caught Sebastian's disapproving expression.

He motioned to their hotel. "Mind if I head to my room to shower and change?"

"Go for it," she said with a shrug, relieved to finally have some alone time to breathe in the fresh mountain air without the stress of being under Sebastian's watchful eye. "I'll be right behind you."

"If I don't see you in the lobby in an hour, meet me at the restaurant at 6 o'clock. Do you remember where the Mandolin is?"

She focused straight ahead, fighting the urge to roll her eyes. "You mean the restaurant *right* across the street from our hotel?"

He twisted a lock of his hair above his ear, tilted his head to the side, and looked at her dolefully—his way of pouting. "You know what I mean. Punctuality isn't your strong suit. Can you make it there by six?"

Mariah waved a hand in the air dismissively and laughed.

Laughing off his coarseness was more effective for improving her mood than fighting with him. He was a decent boyfriend, for the most part. No *one* man had it all. The only perfect man was the one she'd conjured up in her mind and daydreamed about on slow, rainy days. Dang romance novels. Corn dogs and sunny beaches existed, not the perfect man. "I'll be there. Go get showered."

The black iron streetlights blinked on, but the skies were still a good hour away from darkening. Mariah wiggled her bottom on the tiny bike seat and pedaled hard, attempting to ride hands-free. She hadn't ridden a bike without her hands in ages. She lifted her arms at her sides, pumped the pedals, and flew down the road like a kid again. Childlike euphoria tickled her senses.

The front tire wobbled. Beach cruisers were completely different than mountain bikes. Mountain bikes had more... give, somehow. Her rental bike bounced when she hit bumps, absorbing the shock. She grabbed her handlebars and leaned forward, firming her grip. "Let's see what you can do, fancy mountain bike," she said, racing toward a lip in the sidewalk. It took her less than a second to realize her critical error. She didn't have time to slow down or get the adequate lift necessary to clear the curb. Or maybe she simply had no idea what she was doing.

Two seconds later, her body splayed out on the sidewalk, bloody and bruised, but she was still alive. Door chimes jingled in the background, reminding her that Christmas wasn't far off.

CHAPTER TWO

"*A*re you okay?" A man's deep voice warmed her center as he kneeled next to her. "You took at nasty fall." His voice echoed in her head.

Pressing her fingertips to her temple, she sat up, willing her head to stop spinning. The handsome stranger came into focus. The guy had a rugged, yet pretty face, with high cheekbones and a square chin. His eyes were a smoky blue, the color of Bear Lake on a cloudy day. His skin glowed with a fresh tan. She'd seen his face before—in her dreams.

How hard did I hit my head? "Is this real?" she whispered aloud to herself, not able to break her gaze from the gorgeous man.

His blue eyes sparkled. "Unfortunately, I think it is," he said, holding up his phone and shining a light in her eyes. "Where does it hurt?"

"Nowhere," she said with a slow bat of her lashes. Men usually didn't notice her until they looked into her eyes.

She waited for a reaction. None. Perhaps he wasn't a normal man. Perhaps, he'd been sent down from heaven to welcome her into the next life.

I'm dead! she screamed inside. "You're my...?"

"Guardian angel?" He shook his head.

Super-hot soulmate, a gift from heaven, the only thing worth dying for. "Uh-huh," she managed to say.

His eyes lowered, lending a humble expression. "I've heard that one before and believe me, I'm no angel."

Tender hearted rebel. Yep, he's not real. I'm in a coma. "It's nice to know that my fall didn't kill me, just made my brain create a seriously hot guy to suppress the pain."

His face brightened. "That's a first," he said with an amused smile. He placed his hand behind her head for support. "Let me help you inside. Once the sun sets, it'll be freezing out here, and you're not dressed for the cold." He slipped his arm under her legs and effortlessly lifted her, proving he wasn't real, but his warm arms sure felt real.

She rested her forehead on his shoulder. He smelled like the hallway outside of the men's shower room at the swim and tennis club, a mixture of chlorine and pine-scented body wash. Was she in a coma on her way to the hospital? She needed to wake up. She pinched his rock-hard bicep.

His attention shot to his arm. "Ouch," he yelped out. He caught her eye and laughed. His deep belly rumble sent flutters down her side. "I think that only works if you pinch yourself." He carried her into a shoe store and laid her onto a padded bench.

Her eyes went wide. "You're telling me this is real?"

A smile tugged at the corners of his lips. "Let me guess. You realized you weren't dreaming when I brought you into a running store." He kneeled next to her. "Don't worry. I won't judge. Running isn't for everyone. Let me know when you're ready to sit up."

She closed her eyes and rubbed her temples. "This is either fate or the universe is mocking me."

He sat on the wood floor in front of her. She grew

increasingly uncomfortable with his inquisitive stare. He studied her as if they'd met before. "Fate?" he asked.

"Just before I fell, I was thinking about how I needed to purchase a pair of high-quality trail runners." *Oh, and I thought about you—the man of my dreams.*

He stood. Her eyes traced his tall, toned body. He didn't have the typical runners' thin, toned physique. His muscles were bulkier, like the male swim coaches from the swim and tennis club when they demonstrated to their students the proper way to do the butterfly stroke.

Mariah imagined pool water rippling over his back muscles. The air in the room became hot and thin, causing her head to spin again.

The guy caught her eye and glanced down at his chest, then lifted his chin ever so slightly, letting her know he was okay with her checking him out. "I like the idea of you being predestined to come into the store today, but maybe not in your current condition." He snapped his fingers. "Hold tight. I'll grab my bag."

"In my *condition?*" Mariah asked, hoping he didn't think she was a complete loon-bat for pinching him, then checking him out like a love-crazed teenager.

"Bloody." He clarified, motioning to the road rash on her arms and legs before disappearing behind a door at the back of the store.

The mention of blood brought her injuries to the forefront of her mind. Wet warmth prickled her arms and legs. She sat up and did a full body check. As she examined the long, red raspberry road rash down the side of her leg, memories of childhood bike wrecks filled her mind. More than a few times, she'd pulled herself off the pavement in tears.

She slid her legs across the white micro-fiber couch, causing blood to streak the smooth covering.

Embarrassment heated her face. She wouldn't have allowed her cute dream guy to lay her on the bench if she'd known she'd stain it. Is that why he wanted to bandage her up, to prevent her from bleeding all over the store? She stumbled to her feet.

"Hold on," he said, hurrying to her side. He took her hand and had her sit back down. "You're still bleeding."

"That's why I'm leaving. I don't want to stain anything else."

"Don't worry about that," he said, opening his first-aid bag. "I haven't caught your name or where you're visiting from."

"Mariah Larkin. Sacramento."

"Mariah. Beautiful name. I'm Levi. That's thoughtful of you to want to bleed outside, but not smart."

Her eyes narrowed. He did *not* just say that. No one had ever called her stupid before.

His eyes shot to the window with a view of the street. "Do you know what kind of wild animals we get around here?"

Wild forests had been her playground as a child. She swallowed down the rising laugh in her throat. *"Wild animals?"* she said with wide eyes, playing along.

He took her injured leg in his hands and began applying a gooey ointment. She marveled at his soft touch, considering his hands held the rugged and calloused appearance of manual labor.

"If you go outside before I bandage you up, you'll be asking an animal to hunt you down."

He wanted to keep her there longer. But why? Did he feel the same energy between them that she did, or did he simply want to sell her a pair of running shoes to meet his monthly quota? Whatever his motives, she didn't care. She hadn't been this amused in ages and she wasn't about to leave before she understood why her heart rhythm went from half notes to quarter notes every time Levi's hand brushed against her leg.

She bit at her lower lip and furrowed her brow. "You think I'm in danger?" she asked with an exaggerated swallow.

"A city girl like yourself needs to be cautious here at dusk. That's when the wild cats hunt."

Her dad had said something similar when she'd left for California. *Be cautious. Cities are dangerous places.*

Once her bandages were secure, Levi sprang to his feet, ran outside, and returned with her rental bike. "You can leave your bike in here overnight. I'll drive you back to your hotel." He motioned to the far wall which held shelves of colorful running shoes. "When you pick up your bike tomorrow, we'll find your perfect fit."

Sales guy. She knew how to talk his language. "I thought I was looking at him," she said, then caught his intrigued expression. His light blue eyes danced with desire. She cursed the rising heat in her cheeks. She was a sucker for a good one-liner and fell for the salesman type every time. She was falling for Levi's charms, just like she had with Sebastian. *Sebastian! I can't flirt with the cute local.* She had a boyfriend, a boyfriend who was waiting for her. She glanced at the clock on the wall. 5:46. She needed to be at the restaurant in less than fifteen minutes.

"I can't believe I forgot," she blurted out, jumping to her feet.

"Forgot what?"

She patted her hips as if searching her pockets for her car keys. "I have a boyfriend."

"You forgot you have a *boyfriend*?" he asked with a voice of concern. By his confused facial expression, she'd reaffirmed to him how extremely *not* smart she was.

She laughed nervously. "I guess I hit my head harder than I thought."

His eyes traced her face. "Your pupils are dilated. Maybe you should sit a little longer."

"Can't. Already late."

He scrutinized her again, like he had when he first set her on the couch. "You look familiar. Have you been to Sun Valley before?"

"Nope." She covered her blushing cheeks and hurried to the door. "I grew up in Strawberry Falls. Up north. Probably never heard of it. Right?"

"Wish I had. Sounds beautiful," he said, following close behind her.

She held down a snort. "It's no Sun Valley. I left ten years ago today, on my eighteenth birthday."

Levi clapped his hands. "It's your birthday today? You need to celebrate."

She pivoted around to face him. "My boyfriend's waiting for me at the Mandolin. He doesn't like it when I'm late."

Anger flashed across Levi's face. "Doesn't *like* it?"

She blinked, trying to come up with a way to explain Sebastian's cheekiness, but she couldn't find the words and she didn't want to sound like a simpleton, again.

Levi placed his hand on her shoulder. "You were in a bike accident. I think he'll understand if you're a few minutes late." His voice lightened but his jaw didn't relax to match his softened voice. "Wait here. I'll grab my car and run you to the Mandolin." He placed a set of keys in her hands. "The bronze key locks the front door," he said, running outside before she could protest.

The cold air bit at her legs, causing them to stiffen. It took less than ten seconds for her teeth to begin chattering. Yep, bad idea to wear Lycra shorts and a tank top on a frosty fall day in Idaho. By the time she'd secured the two dead bolts, Levi had pulled up to the curb in a BMW SUV.

At least with how he bandaged me up I won't bleed on his fancy leather seat, she thought, climbing into his car. "I'm not exactly in fine-dining attire," she said with a sigh.

"Do you want me to take you to your hotel so you can change?" he asked, pulling out into traffic.

"That would be great. We have separate rooms at the Sleepy Inn." She'd felt compelled to tell him that she and Sebastian were staying in separate rooms. But why? She didn't owe him an explanation. She scolded herself for offering unsolicited personal information. "It's three blocks down, on the right."

His shoulders relaxed. "Thanks," he said with a friendly wink, letting her know he was familiar with the area.

Idiot, she scolded herself. Telling him how to get to her hotel would be like him telling her how to get around Strawberry Falls.

"Here we are," he said, pulling to the curb of the Sleepy Inn.

"We're here already?" she said, placing her hand on the passenger door handle but she couldn't bring herself to open the door. She feared the comfort of Levi's presence would be yanked from her the moment she stepped out of his car.

"Oh. Sorry. Where are my manners?" he said as if she were waiting for him to help her out of the car. He jumped out, ran around his car, and opened her door. "I'll wait for you in the lobby," he said, taking her hand.

"You don't need to—"

"I know," he said, helping her out of the car. "But you hit your head and I wouldn't feel right leaving you alone. I'll personally deliver you to your boyfriend for him to watch over you."

Watch over me? Sebastian had never been the nursing type. "Thanks for doctoring me up," she said.

Levi held open the glass door to the inn. "It's what I do," he said, motioning for her to go inside. "I'm an EMT.

Paramedic. When I volunteered with the LA Fire Department, I saw a lot of trauma. These days, I jump out of airplanes most days to fight forest fires."

Her chest burned, but she didn't know why. Admiration? Wonder? Desire? Maybe all three. She envisioned him running through hot embers toward smoking trees, his handsome face streaked with black ash. She had to know more about why he chose to risk his life to save the forest. She pressed her hand against the cold glass and closed the door, shutting them outside. He released the door handle and stepped back.

She leaned against the door, preventing him from opening it again. "You *what?*"

He stared into her eyes with an expression of satisfaction. "My road to becoming a smokejumper is a long story. I'll tell you about it tomorrow when you come into the store." He stepped closer, causing her throat to dry and the air to catch in her lungs as if she were running through flames—or toward them. If he leaned down to kiss her, she wasn't sure if she'd stop him. His pool and pine scent filled her senses. *Strike that.* She wasn't sure if he could stop *her* from kissing him. He brushed his hand along her right side at her waist. She leaned toward him, closed her eyes, and…waited.

Time paused until the metal door handle clicked behind her back. She released her held breath and stepped to the side as Levi pulled open the Inn's front door.

He spoke quietly into her ear. "Right now, you're late for your birthday date. We have tomorrow. I'm not going anywhere."

Disappointment settled in her gut. Waiting until tomorrow to know his secrets would be torturous. Cool air rushed past them into the hotel lobby decorated in a modern lodge motif. The fireplace beckoned her, but she walked toward the elevator. "What if you're called up to fight a forest fire tomorrow?"

He shook his head. "Seasonal wildland firefighters are off the clock until April."

The elevator doors opened. Mariah stepped inside and pushed the button for the third floor, although there was no more going up for her; Levi had sent her soaring higher than she'd ever been before. "I'll be back down in less than five minutes." She leaned against the metal elevator wall and smiled as the doors closed out the best thing she'd ever experienced in Idaho.

"Levi." She whispered the word so softly that it tickled the inside of her lips.

Her phone vibrated inside her arm sleeve. A call was coming in from her dad. His sixth sense was spot on, once again. Her dad always seemed to call when she needed him the most, and she didn't want his call to drop while she was inside the elevator. She sent him an auto message that she'd call him back. She needed expert advice from the one person whom she'd seen do relationships right. When she'd asked him how she would know if she should marry Sebastian, he'd told her that if she had to ask, then she shouldn't even consider marrying him. No need to rush it. He'd tried to explain to her what it would feel like to be so madly in love with someone that no one else existed. He'd told her that if the hottest guy in the world walked into the room, she'd notice him, but not bat an eyelash in his direction. After meeting Levi, she finally understood what love *wasn't*, because she *had* noticed the hottest guy in the world. She hadn't batted *an* eyelash in his direction; she'd batted *every single one*.

Calm settled over her. She finally knew for certain that Sebastian wasn't the man for her. The real question: how to tell him. She couldn't break up with him while he ate the one thing which brought him true enjoyment, but she had to do it—and soon. She tapped her teeth in thought. She'd tell him in the morning. There was no reason to ruin his favorite meal *and* her birthday.

The elevator dinged for the third floor. Idaho sure had improved over the past decade. *Twenty-eight*—not bad for a new lucky number.

CHAPTER THREE

*T*he tall grandfather clock in the corner of the hotel lobby came to life, chiming six times. Levi paced the zebra printed rug in front of the gas fireplace.

He couldn't tell Mariah why she looked so familiar. She'd either think he was coming on to her or that he was a lunatic. With her stunning violet eyes, she'd most certainly heard every pick-up line in the book. Her eyes were rare, but he'd seen those very same eyes before, many, many times. It wasn't just her brilliant eye color that had him staring; Mariah had the same perfect nose, full lips, and creamy white skin as the woman he called Aunt Char. The real zinger—she even shared the same suppressed giggle for a laugh…but it wasn't possible.

The elevator doors opened. Mariah stepped out wearing a black backless gown that flowed over her curves like a chocolate fountain with the hem brushing her ankles. She turned in a circle. "What do you think?"

Levi metaphorically picked his tongue up off the floor. He'd been attracted to Mariah at the running store, but he'd been in his life-saving medic-mode then; he'd kept their interaction professional. Now, she glowed with seductive confidence. Thankfully, his attraction to her didn't feel uncomfortable. Aunt Char and the Terrences were as close as family but there was no blood relation between them.

Seeing Mariah in her evening gown brought back his previous pretentious life. He hadn't missed anything about LA, until now. Trendy social gatherings which hosted lavishly dressed, beautiful aspiring actresses in search of a billionaire husband had been a huge part of his life. Shamefully, he'd entertained those beautiful women's advances until he'd realized that he was the one being played. Then the scare happened.

Levi cleared his throat when he realized Mariah was waiting for him to answer her question. "You look amazing."

Her cheeks blushed a vibrant shade of pink and her eyes dipped to the floor bashfully. "Thanks, but I wasn't soliciting a compliment. I was asking if my bandages were visible. I don't want everyone to know how clumsy I am."

He pulled open the front door. "Believe me, clumsy won't be the word on people's lips tonight when they look at you."

A soft smile played at her lips. "And what word *will* they be thinking?"

Either his radar was jacked, or she was flirting with him. "Still not soliciting a compliment?" He teased, taking her by the arm. "And you're not exactly dressed for the weather," he said, trying to not stare at how her dress hung off her shoulders and scooped low down her back. "I thought you'd come out in a parka and snow boots."

"What's the fun in that?" She pressed her fingertips to her lips and giggled in her throat.

"Uncanny," he said, helping her into his SUV and closing the passenger side door.

Her laughter only grew as he ran around to the driver's side. He turned away and checked his fly. Not down. He settled into his seat and caught her amused expression. She didn't even try to hide the fact that she was laughing at him. "What's so funny?" he asked, pressing the ignition button.

Mariah glanced at her hotel. "If you don't figure it out in a minute, I'll tell you."

Was something comical about her hotel? He pulled out into the street, flipped a U-turn at the light, then parked in front of the Mandolin, exactly across the street from the Sleepy Inn. They could've walked across the street in less time than it took him to drive them there. "Oh," he said, leaning back in his seat and feeling like a complete idiot. This girl had gotten up in his head and caused all sorts of trouble.

She wrinkled her nose playfully. "And I thought *I'd* turned into a city girl."

He tilted his head back against his headrest. "Just the type of thing you'd expect from a Harvard Law graduate and corporate attorney who'd managed billions in capital venture funds."

Mariah's laughter faded and her eyes narrowed. He'd hoped to impress her with his credentials. By her steely reaction, he'd done the opposite. That line had always worked before. His game was off tonight, or maybe she wasn't attracted to the corporate, rich type. He backpedaled. "I practiced law in my past life."

Mariah's eyes followed her hand as she slid her fingers down her arm rest. "Shoe salesman," she said more to herself than to him.

"Shoe salesman?" He wasn't sure why that had offended him. He was, in fact, a shoe salesman, but he was also an attorney, a businessman, a smokejumper, and a billionaire. If she wanted a shoe salesman, that's exactly what he'd be. Time to own it. "I sure am. The best shoe salesman you've ever met. And I'll show you tomorrow."

Mariah looked anxiously at the restaurant while she rubbed her forehead. "I'm not sure I'll be needing—"

"That's right," Levi said hurriedly. He bounced out of the car and ran around to help her out. He found her standing on the curb, waiting for him. "I forgot you're late for your birthday date with your boyfriend." He waited to see if she would say something to give him hope…anything. Her face registered concern—not the best sign.

She bit at her lip nervously while she rocked back and forth from her heels to her toes. "Thanks for helping me," she said, patting her thigh where he'd applied the largest bandage. Truth be told, she would've been fine if she'd simply scrubbed off the grit from her tumble with a little soap and warm water. "And thanks for making sure I got here safely."

"You're not inside yet," he said, offering her his arm. "I promised to deliver you personally to your boyfriend."

Mariah cringed but accepted his arm. Levi couldn't remember the last time a woman flinched at his touch, if ever. Did she recoil because of his Harvard comment? If she weren't into him, he would accept that, but he couldn't let her out of his sight, not yet. He needed to know why she looked like a young Aunt Char.

A new hostess stood behind the tall mahogany welcome desk. She smiled courteously as they entered. By her unaffected, relaxed appearance, she didn't recognize Levi. Relief washed over him. He didn't know how Mariah would react if she knew his family owned the restaurant.

The college-aged hostess dipped her chin and said, "Welcome to the Mandolin. Do you have a reservation with us tonight?"

Mariah motioned to the far corner of the room, past the piano. "My friend's already here." Her eyes connected with Levi's.

Internal fist bump. She'd said friend, not boyfriend. That one word gave Levi reason to hope.

The man sitting at the far corner table waved Mariah over. She acknowledged him with a blink, then turned back to Levi. "This place is amazing! Chic French décor, soft candlelight lighting, and there's even a live pianist playing French bistro music. I feel like I'm in France again," she said, reaching up and giving Levi a peck on his cheek. "I'll stop by the running store tomorrow to pick up the bike. Thanks for everything."

He pointed at his chest. "Shoe salesman." Her eyes danced with amusement while she giggled in her throat. *Shoe salesman? That's the best you got? You idiot!* he chastised himself. Mariah sauntered across the dining room, gracefully dodging a waiter who carried a tray of food. Levi's respirations quickened. *Nope, clumsy wouldn't be the word to describe her.* A few feet before she reached her boyfriend's table, she glanced back at him and smiled, warming him deep in his bones. He rested his arm on the welcoming table and breathed out a happy sigh.

"Sir," said the hostess in a commanding voice. "Would you like a seat at the bar?"

He glanced at her name tag. "Joy, it's a pleasure to meet you. I'm Levi Grant."

Deer in the headlights would be an understatement for her shocked, mortified, yet equally flirtatious reaction. "I thought that I'd met all of the Grant brothers."

"How long have you been working here?"

"Six months."

He ran his fingers through his hair. "Has it really been that long?" he asked himself. He'd been fighting forest fires a long time. It was good to be back. The Mandolin had been his second home growing up. When he wasn't in his mom's kitchen at home, he was at the family restaurant. Other than

23

occasional staffing adjustments, the Mandolin was the one place that never changed. He always got a cozy feeling when he walked in through the front door and smelled the aroma of freshly baked baguettes.

"Yeah, it's been a while," said Joy, answering his rhetorical question. "I started working here at the end of ski season."

"I see," he said. Drones of seasonal employees drifted in and out of Sun Valley, but his family usually employed locals who wouldn't bail during slack, the off season between the summer and winter months. He'd left seven months ago, in March to ready the equipment to train the new recruits, so it made sense he hadn't met the new hostess. "Have any of my brothers been in tonight?"

"Yeah," she said, pointing to a server with his back to them in black slacks and a blue button-up shirt. "Andrew, right? He said he's just in town for the day."

"Andy?" Levi said with excitement. "He's been on the circuit. We haven't seen each other in months." He took a step forward to greet his brother but was stopped when Joy grabbed hold of his arm and yanked him back. "That's quite a grip you have there," he said, hoping she'd release him gracefully.

"I'm so impressed by you and your brothers. Andrew could be racing down the street right now, flirting with all the fancy celebrities in town. Instead, he's here because we're shorthanded tonight."

"That *Andrew* is quite a guy. You keep your eyes on *him*," he said with an encouraging nod.

"Really," she said with a little hop of excitement.

He carefully shimmied out of her grasp. "Really. All he needs is a little encouragement. Excuse me, while I go speak with him." She pulled her hand back, allowing him to make a beeline for Andy.

He walked up behind Andy as he was entering the

kitchen. He threw his arms around his brother and lifted him up from behind, cracking a few bones in his back.

Andy grunted, then spun around with a laugh and embraced Levi. "Man, I've missed you." He threw a fist into Levi's chest. "Every time I see you, you turn more into Mr. Universe."

"Quit, you're embarrassing me in front of the kitchen staff," said Levi, motioning around the chrome kitchen, but everyone was too busy with what they were working on in front of them to look up. "What are you doing in town? I thought you were racing this weekend."

"I am but my NASCAR race isn't until Sunday. I flew in for the day in the hopes of celebrating Mom and Dad's thirtieth wedding anniversary with them. With Mom fawning over her first grandchild, I haven't seen her all summer." His face dropped. "I didn't know they were in Africa on a safari."

"Dad surprised Mom last minute with the trip. They flew out two days ago. How'd you get roped into working tonight?"

Andy scratched the side of his face. "I had nothing to do and a waiter called in sick. This restaurant is more home than anyplace else to me."

"I hear ya, bro."

"Want some food?" Andy asked, holding up his notepad.

"Not hungry."

"Then why are *you* here tonight?"

Levi opened the swinging kitchen door. "See that girl at table number twelve?"

"Ah-ha!" Andy laughed out as he stuck an order on the rotating wheel for the chef. "It always comes down to a girl with you. Doesn't it?"

"I'm serious. Did you *see* her?"

Andy's teasing smile disappeared. "I didn't take a good

look at her, but her boyfriend is a piece of work. Guess what he told her when I was taking their drink order." He paused as if Levi were actually going to guess.

Levi held up his hands. "Dude, seriously. What?"

"He said that most men would expect intimacy on a weekend retreat like this. Something about how he felt she didn't respect him because she showed up late for dinner. I wanted to deck the guy."

"You should've." The words ground out of Levi's mouth. "Or maybe I'll do it."

"Whoa, cowboy," said Andy, grabbing the back of Levi's shirt. "Who *is* this woman?"

"Someone I met today." Levi lowered his voice. "I need you to take a closer look at her, then tell me if I'm going crazy."

"Alright. But are you thinking what I'm thinking?" Andy asked, lifting an appetizer platter in the air. "I need another one of these, Joe!" he yelled to a cook in the back. Joe waved a hand in the air but didn't raise his eyes.

Levi nodded. "I'm one hundred and fifty percent with you."

Andy stepped out of the kitchen. "Good thing lawyers don't need math skills. Come to the bar with me while I get their drinks."

Levi sat at the bar and watched as Andy wove his way with two drinks and the appetizer platter to Mariah's table.

CHAPTER FOUR

"*T*his reminds me of the Orsay Museum in Paris," said Mariah, staring at an Impressionist-inspired painting of a wheat field which hung on the mustard wall next to their table. "Fresh air and light, that's what this painting says to me. What does it say to you?"

The frown on Sebastian's face told her he wasn't ready to forgive her for being late and kissing a man's cheek in the restaurant's lobby who'd "saved her bacon," as she'd phrased it. She could have refrained from praising Levi, but she didn't see the point in that. Sebastian had asked who she'd walked in with. He would've seen right through her if she'd lied or downplayed her respect for the man who'd carried her inside the shoe store and bandaged her up. When Levi had said he was a Harvard Law graduate and managed billions of dollars for other people, it threw her. She hadn't pegged him for the covetous type

The waiter placed a huge plate in front of her. "In celebration of your birthday today, the chef will be preparing a special five course meal for you, on the house."

Mariah's hand flew to her chest. "That's so kind," she said, staring down at the plate of snails with green butter, stuffed squid, chunky rare beef, and some type of liver pate. She never would have chosen an appetizer platter with that combination, but she was up for an adventure.

Sebastian's face lifted into a suspicious smile. "Mariah, there's something to say for how your beguiling eyes help you make new friends." He turned his attention to the waiter. "Will our meal be chosen for us, then, or should we order?"

"Beguiling eyes?" the waiter asked, ignoring Sebastian's question. He leaned down to within a few inches of Mariah's face and stared into her eyes. "Stunning, but the candlelight doesn't do them justice." He held up a finger. "But candlelight is great for romantic dinner photos. Would you like me to snap a few photos of you two?"

Sebastian handed the waiter his phone. "Yes. Thank you."

Mariah didn't have any interest in remembering her last "romantic" dinner with Sebastian and couldn't muster a smile.

The waiter snapped a few shots, then gave Sebastian's phone back to him. "One more for good measure," he said, taking a phone out of his own pocket and holding it high above his head to include himself in the selfie. "To new friends."

Levi's gorgeous face popped into Mariah's mind, warming her heart, and helping her find her smile.

"New friends?" Sebastian muttered out his annoyance at the waiter's comment. "So, you don't need to take our order, then?"

The waiter pocketed his phone and whipped out a notepad. "Tonight's complimentary meal is for the beguiling birthday girl. But I'm happy to take your order, sir."

Mariah zoned out Sebastian's snarky come-back while she picked up a stuffed squid and popped it into her mouth. A bouquet of savory saffron and cream exploded in her mouth. The bite was firm yet moist, creating the perfect balance.

The waiter left the table, leaving Sebastian with a scowl on his face.

"Sebastian, this is amazing, you have to try this," she said, placing a stuffed squid on his bread plate.

Sebastian's top lip quivered. "What's going on with you and that waiter? And then there's your shoe salesman hero?" he asked in a suggestive tone.

It was time. She hadn't planned on ending it this quickly, but he gave her no choice. "Nothing, Sebastian. The first time I ever saw that waiter was when he asked for our drink order. But you're right to feel like something is off between us. I didn't realize it until today, but it's time for us to reframe our relationship."

"Reframe?" Sebastian said in anger. "You can't mean that."

She maintained a serious expression, not upset, or angry, or sad...serious, like she meant business. "I'm sorry."

Sweat beaded across Sebastian's brow. He pushed the appetizer plate aside and took her hands in his. "You and me make sense, Mariah," he said, giving her hands a light squeeze. "I'll do anything to keep you. Look at what I've already done to make you happy," he said, glancing around the restaurant. "You won't ever need to work again. Let me pamper you, take care of you so you won't ever want for anything."

She pulled her hands back. "I can only offer you my friendship, Sebastian. That's if you still want to be friends."

His shoulders slumped and his fingers found the lock of hair above his ear. "Will you still hike the Grand Canyon with me?"

"Sebastian..." Her eyes dropped to her plate. She couldn't look at him when he pouted, or she'd cave.

"As friends," he added.

"Are you sure that's a good idea?" she asked, worried he wasn't taking their break-up seriously. "You're okay with us spending that much time together knowing we're no longer a couple?" He flinched as if she'd flung kitchen knives at him. "I'm not trying to hurt you, Sebastian. That's why I'm telling you this. I want to be honest with you. You're a good man and I'll look back at our time together with fondness. Here, have a snail," she said, placing a snail on his plate. "Let's not talk about this anymore. I want you to enjoy your meal."

He perked up slightly as he dug the snail out of its shell with a tiny fork and gulped it down with a moan.

She couldn't get the childhood memory of pouring salt on garden snails out of her head. She coughed, willing her stomach to quit churning. "In fact, have all the snails," she said, pushing the appetizer plate toward him. "I'll wait for the French onion soup."

The rest of the evening went surprisingly smooth. She'd never thought a break-up could be so amicable, enjoyable even. They chatted with ease the remainder of the meal before walking back to the Sleepy Inn.

Mariah said goodnight to Sebastian and opened her hotel room door. A foot into the room, a white envelope rested on the diamond-patterned carpet. Check-out bill, she thought, opening the letter. It read, Balance for your stay, Zero. Happy Birthday, Mariah. Please visit with us again soon.

"You've got to be kidding me," she said, plopping onto the bed, unsure if she felt gratitude or a sense of indebtedness. Other than Sebastian, the only other person in town who knew it was her birthday was Levi. Why would he pay for her meal and her hotel? Even more pressing: what did he want from her? She hated having to wait until tomorrow to ask him.

Levi's warm breath on her ear, telling her he wasn't going anywhere, carried her through her bedtime routine of washing her face, brushing her teeth, and slipping on her warm pajamas. She jumped into bed with her iPad, typed Levi into the Google browser, and hit enter. The only sites that popped up were for blue jeans, of course. She should've asked Levi his last name. The only thing she knew about him was that he'd been an attorney once and now worked in a shoe store when he wasn't fighting wildfires. A zip of energy caused her to sit up taller. She typed wildland firefighter into her browser. She garnered from her quick search that wildland firefighters worked for the US Forest Service, the more elite crews were hotshots and smokejumpers.

Within seconds, a short documentary about a hotshot crew loaded on her browser and began playing. Tears tumbled down her cheeks as wives spoke about losing their husbands, and parents lamented over the loss of their sons. The entire crew, minus one? Unable to comprehend the loss, Mariah paused the video.

An add popped up for a full-feature film, Hollywood's version of the events. The trailer looked promising, uplifting even. Falling asleep to a heart-warming story of hope and resilience was exactly what she needed tonight.

Mariah spent the next hour laughing and cheering on the wildland firefighters in their quest to become elite. Then the fire blazed on her screen; her body reacted in opposition, turning cold and clammy. Her chest tightened and tears poured from her eyes as she gasped for air. She fell into a restless sleep while images of charred bodies, smoking trees, and wailing widows haunted her dreams.

CHAPTER FIVE

*T*he next morning, she lay in bed, downtrodden and lacking a single spit of energy. She blamed her tiredness on the long bike ride yesterday. If she blamed it on anything else, then she'd be admitting that Levi could share the same fate as those unfortunate firefighters.

She snuggled her face into her pillow, blocking out the morning light. "I really liked him." Her voice muffled into her pillow. It was as if she were saying goodbye to Levi in anticipation for his last run-in with the forest's flames.

Her stomach gurgled. Her father's voice told her to eat healthy and get outside, pushing her out of bed. Enough whining, she told herself. Levi was alive. She would eat breakfast, go to the running store, buy trail running shoes, then ride away on her rental bike, never to see Levi, the super-hot and kind wildland firefighter, again. She didn't belong in a place where handsome strangers paid for her birthday meal. She belonged in California, where handsome strangers stole her birthday meal as she strolled down the boardwalk. She'd take the transient muggers if they came as a package deal with the ocean. She needed the calming waves to quiet her unsettled heart.

After a quick shower and light cosmetic application to combat her red, puffy eyes, she slipped on drawstring jogger pants and a loose, long-sleeved yoga shirt. Comfort was key on a metaphorically cloudy day.

The skies were crystal clear. Clear as a Montana sunrise, as her mom, a Montana native, would say. She stepped out onto the sidewalk of the Sleepy Inn and breathed in the crisp mountain air; grateful the suffocating smoke didn't linger outside of her mind. She cupped her hand over her irritated eyes, blocking out the harsh morning light.

With a spring in her step, she sang her favorite Johnny Cash song "I Can See Clearly Now," quietly to herself to combat her unease. Friendly strangers passed her on the sidewalk, humming to their own melodies. There was something about the mountains and fresh air that made people neighborly and kind. She rubbed her neck while she glanced up at the mountain peaks in awe at their splendor. Perhaps it was the beautiful trees with their changing leaves that had everyone in such a good mood. The sunlight hit the mountainside, illuminating the red and yellow leaves, creating the illusion of bursting flames.

Trees are fuel! roared through Mariah's mind like a rushing locomotive, causing her to stumble as her toes caught the sidewalk. She regained her footing, avoiding another embarrassing spill, but her eyes never left the mountainside; she saw the colorful forest through new eyes. The trees were at the ready. All they needed was a single spark to ignite their kindling and an unstoppable fire would sweep down the mountainside and decimate Sun Valley and Ketchum.

Note to self: never watch another firefighter movie. And never ever, ever date a wildland firefighter.

"Shoes," she said, barreling into the running store, flustered and out of breath.

"Mariah?" Levi said with a questioning expression as if he weren't expecting her.

"I won't bug you for long. I'm just looking for a good pair of trail walking shoes, then I'll be out of your hair," she said with resolution.

"I'm glad you made it in. Give me one minute to finish up here, then I'll be right with you."

A pack of trend-setting teens scanned Mariah in one swoop before returning to their one-sided conversations, talking more into their phones than to each other. They buzzed out of the store like a swarm of honeybees, sniffing out their next meal, leaving Mariah and Levi to stare at each other in awkward silence.

Levi scratched the side of his chin and looked at her as if he'd asked her a question and was awaiting her answer.

"Did I come at a bad time?" she asked.

He blinked. "Where do you plan to trail run?" he asked, walking over to a treadmill, and turning it on.

"I'm setting a New Year's resolution to hike the Grand Canyon, rim to rim in a day."

"Impressive," he said, motioning for her to jump up onto the treadmill. "That's a great goal. I've been wanting to do that hike myself."

She took a step back. "I'm sorry. Did you want me to go on that machine for some reason?"

"Sorry," he said with a wave of his hand and a wrinkled brow. "My head has been a little off lately. Let me explain what we do here. We first do a gait analysis," he said, stepping onto the treadmill. "We test pronation, the degree at which your foot rolls when you run." The belt sped. "Watch how I run."

"You want me to stare at your legs?" she asked, cursing

the heat rising up her neck. Don't look at his hot legs, she told herself, focusing on his eyes. His glorious blue eyes. Dang, that backfired.

A smile split his lips. "Look at my feet. Do you see how they roll slightly inward as I run?"

She nodded.

"That means I have over pronation or low arches. If my feet had rolled outward that would've meant I'd have under pronation or have high arches. Someone who doesn't roll at all has a neutral pronate." He lowered the speed and jumped off the treadmill. "Your turn."

Her fingernails found their way to her teeth. "No judgment?" she asked, meandering toward the death machine while she bit down on her nails. Swimming and occasional yoga were her thing; running had never been part of her repertoire of exercises. She hadn't been known to be quick and nimble on the track, quite the opposite. She was about to have another most embarrassing moment and there was nothing she could do to stop it.

"No judgment," he repeated with a laugh.

She smacked his arm. "You just laughed at me. That's judgment."

"I laughed at your face," he said, taking her hand to encourage her onto the treadmill.

"Excuse me?" she said, acting offended as she stepped up onto the machine.

He clipped a red stop-cord to her shirt at her belly. "I was laughing at your facial expression. It was cute. Your smile lights up the room, but your sassy facial expression warms the soul."

She found herself getting reeled in by Levi like a flopping fish. Whose soul? She wanted to ask in a flirtatious voice. Don't fall for the salesman's one-liners, Mariah, she counseled herself as the treadmill's belt sped up under her feet. Her pace settled in at a light jog.

Levi stepped behind the treadmill. Having him watch her body giggle for a minute was more painful than being in the dentist's chair for an hour. While she ran, the question kept running through her mind. *Why did he pay my bills last night?*

With a hearty clap, he said, "That's it."

She stopped running, but the belt kept travelling. Her adrenaline spiked. The cord went taught, ultimately snapping from the machine, and causing the belt to halt. She stumbled and spun, bracing for impact with the floor, but Levi caught her around the waist and held her steady.

"Thanks," she panted out, grateful to be in Levi's arms again. With her on the treadmill, and him standing eight inches lower on the wood floor, it brought their faces to the same height. His arms continued to hold firm around her back while their eyes connected. She had a blissful moment of staring into Levi's clear blue eyes until he broke the comfortable silence.

"I'm here for you," he said in a soft voice, his lips so close she could taste his minty breath. His words were kind, but it was his eyes which spoke to her. They told her that this is who he was, that he would always be there for those who needed him. He would always be there for her...until the forest flames took him.

"I can't do this," she said in a breathy voice.

His forehead creased. "Do what?"

Fall in love with you! "Treadmills. I'm more of a swimming type of girl."

"Really?" he said with excitement. "Me too."

"Swimming gave you these muscles?" she said, rubbing his shoulder. His body tensed and his respirations quickened; that's when she realized what she'd just done. Biting the inside of her mouth, she stepped down from the treadmill and out of his arms, placing the death machine between them. She'd manhandled Levi. No more risking close proximity, or she might fall even harder.

"My brother's an ex-NFL player. I reached out to him a while back for him to put me on a training schedule. That's part of the long history I was going to tell you, but it's boring. Let's find you some shoes," he said, walking over to the wall of colorful running shoes.

This guy was more mystery than the forest in Poland where the trees grow at a ninety-degree angle. "Why did you do it?"

He shrugged. "Not much to tell. Boring."

She followed behind him. "I mean, why would someone I'd just met pay for my meal and my hotel room last night?"

"Birthdays are big deals in small towns," he said, scratching his neck like he had no idea what she was talking about. "And birthday gifts are just that, gifts. They don't come with an 'I owe you' stamp." His jaw clenched. "No one should ever make you feel like you owe him something when they do something nice for you."

"A gift?" she said with suspicion, picking up a red running shoe that looked like something out of a Seinfeld episode and placed it under her nose. "Can't beat the new shoe smell. It reminds me of shopping trips into the city." She caught his inquisitive stare. "That sounded pretty small-town, didn't it?"

"Believe me," he said, looking out the window. "I understand what it's like to grow up in a small town and pine for the city life. I finally appreciate our little slice of heaven here. I've grown to love small towns in general while protecting them as a smokejumper."

She snapped her fingers, then pointed at him. "That's it, smokejumper. I couldn't remember if you were with the hotshots or the smokejumpers." Shoot, she wasn't going to bring that up. She didn't want to know anything more about him. Strike that. She really wanted to know more about him, but if he opened up to her, she knew she'd fall even harder... to the point of no return.

He raised his left eyebrow. "Smokejumper. AKA adrenaline junkie. An easy way to remember is that I'm the one that jumps out of airplanes to fight wildland fires."

Flashbacks of wailing women and charred remains turned her stomach. She made her way to the white bench, cleaned of her blood, and sat to get off her shaking legs. "So, you first skydive, then you run toward burning trees? Sounds safe enough," she said, laying the sarcasm on thick.

"It all started with me needing to get into shape," he said, grabbing her foot and removing her shoe. Her mind was too occupied to really notice him measuring her foot, but she heard the get into shape comment.

"You needed to get into shape? I'm sorry but I find that hard to believe."

He winked at her, causing her head to go fuzzy. "Because I'm so fit now?"

"Do you really need to ask me that?" she said, waving the heat away from her face with her hand.

"You like red?" he asked, lifting up the red shoe she'd grabbed off the shelf. Honestly, they all looked the same to her, but she did like the color. "This is a great trail runner. You know everything I said about arches? Now, forget it. The most important thing is comfort. I'll be right back with your size." He disappeared into a room at the back of the store, leaving her to wonder why he'd had her run on the treadmill if the only thing that mattered was comfort. And he never told her why he'd had to get into shape.

He returned with four shoe boxes. Before he opened the first box, she asked, "Why would you ever need to get into shape?"

"I had an episode with my heart."

Her hand flew to her mouth. "I'm so sorry."

"It's okay. It has a happy ending. I think," he said, meeting her eyes before he slipped the red running shoe onto her foot. "Two years ago, my childhood crush chose my brother over me. I didn't handle it well. I started working crazy hours as a corporate attorney." He patted his stomach where she could only imagine there had once been a small gut. Now, his abs were rock solid.

She wiped the fresh perspiration from her forehead. "Tell me more."

"Until my scare, I didn't think about how my bad habits were affecting my body. Luckily, I didn't have a full-blown heart attack, but I needed to make some changes. The first thing I did was put one of my brothers in charge of my training and diet. A few months later, I volunteered as a wildland firefighter in the summer and as an EMT with my neighborhood fire department in the winter. I also scaled back my hours at work. With keeping my heart in check and all the running I was doing, it naturally evolved into me opening my own running store where my stress level would be at its lowest. Now, how does that feel?"

"Wonderful. Heart-warming. I'm truly touched by your story. You could've chosen to simply work out at a gym, but you decided to serve your community instead."

His entire face lifted into a broad smile. "Thank you, but I was asking how your foot feels inside that shoe."

"Oh," she said, her eyes lowering to her feet. She hopped up and strolled around the room. Her foot rocked back and forth with an added spring in her step. The shoe molded to her foot like a foamy cushion. "A-plus for comfort."

"Great," he said, motioning to the bench. "Let's get the matching shoe on you and see how they feel together."

Time to find out why he'd really put her on that blasted

running machine. "Do you think I need arch supports, after watching me run?" she said, leaning her side against the treadmill.

"The shoe you picked out already has sufficient support. If it feels comfortable, I wouldn't go any higher."

Her eyes narrowed as she moved to the bench to put on the other shoe. "Then why did you have me run on the treadmill?"

"I used to swear by gait analysis. I haven't been able to completely kick it to the side yet. My sister-in-law is a physical therapist and she schooled me about the dangers of subscribing to the over-promotion of over-pronation."

She wrinkled up her nose while she bent down to tighten her laces. "You lost me."

"Recent studies have shown that the best thing for feet is comfort. It's actually beneficial to run barefoot. You could also practice picking items up with your toes to strengthen them."

She had a sudden urge to take off the huge shoes she'd just put on her feet and test out how well she could lift objects with her toes. Instead, she hopped up and walked around the room. Levi stared at her feet as she zigzagged across the floor. Either he had a thing for feet, or he had a thing for the woman who'd schooled him about them. "Is this physical therapist the one you crushed on?" Hurt surfaced in his eyes, making her wish she'd never asked.

"No. My crush was Hannah. She married my brother, Simon. The therapist's name is Millie and she married my brother, Nathanial, Nate for short. He's the NFL player who whipped me into shape."

She knew she should stop prying but she couldn't stop herself. "What are your brothers' names?" she asked casually as she sat back down on the bench. Time to get Levi's last name and finally know who she was falling for.

He laughed. "You ready for this?" he said, rubbing his palms together and sitting next to her. "There'll be a pop quiz at the end."

She kept her laugh in her throat. "What's my prize if I can recite their names back to you?"

He glanced at his watch. "Lunch?"

"But it's not my birthday today," she said in a coquettish voice. Mariah, stop flirting!

"Which means you don't get a birthday kiss. Your loss."

Mariah's eyes moved over Levi's lips. They opened slightly, beckoning her to kiss them. She swallowed to combat her instant dry mouth.

He looked at her as if he might kiss her, then patted his thigh. "Here we go. The oldest is Simon Peter, then there's me."

"Hold on," she said, stopping him. "Peter is your last name?"

"Grant. You sound like my first-grade teacher. But fine, I'll start again. Simon Peter Grant, Matthew Levi Grant, James Grant, Nathanael Grant, Andrew Grant, John Grant, and Thomas Grant."

There it was, Grant. She whistled. "Seven brothers? And all apostles. Your mother made it easy on me."

He rubbed his chin and blinked. "No one's ever guessed we were named after apostles."

She patted her chest. "I'm from Strawberry Falls. My mama took me to church every Sunday and the leather cover of her Bible is well worn."

"I'm impressed. It's one thing to have a Bible that rests on the coffee table. It's another for its cover to be worn. Alright, Strawberry Falls, let's hear it."

She cleared her throat and sat up straight. "Do the names have to be in order?"

"No, but you get extra points if they are."

"Ooh, extra points." She wiggled her torso and looked up at the ceiling in thought. "Let's see. Okay, Andrew was the oldest apostle, a full year older than Christ and his younger brother, Simon was also an apostle."

"Got two names but not in the right order." He teased her.

She held up her pointer finger. "Not so fast. I never said Andrew came first in your family. You'd said that Simon stole your girl and older brothers tend to do that so I'm gonna go with Simon Peter as the oldest. Next there's Matthew Levi." She held back the urge to wink at him. "That's you. There were two other fisherman brothers, James and John." She closed her eyes and told her mind to remember the order. "I'm going with James next."

"You're golden so far."

"You'd mentioned your brother Nate. Nathanael." Time to guess. "John, Andrew, and Thomas."

"So close!" He slapped his thigh. "I really wanted you to get it. "John and Thomas are the last two, identical twins. Andrew is after Nate." His eyes lit with enjoyment.

The temperature in the room went up a few degrees as she stared into his eyes. She couldn't imagine a man being more attractive than Levi, but maybe there were six other men just as handsome. "And do they all look like you?"

"Uglier. But you tell me. You've met one."

She rubbed her forehead. Her brain was already hurting from trying to remember their names. She ran through the events of the past twenty-four hours and every man she'd met. There weren't many. Shouldn't be too difficult.

"I'll give you a hint," he said, placing his hand over hers on her lap. "He's fast on the track and the oldest apostle."

"Track?" she asked herself. "Does he own the bike rental place?" The guy at the bike shop was blonde, short, and pudgy. He looked nothing like Levi.

"No," Levi laughed out, then held his phone to his mouth. "Nate Grant, NASCAR racer."

"NASCAR racer? When would I have met a—"

Levi held his phone out to her and said, "Remember this guy?"

She recognized his face immediately. "My waiter?" Her waiter had been super cute but all she'd thought about during dinner last night was Levi and how to break up with Sebastian. "I have to admit, his eyes were dreamy." I noticed him, but I didn't bat an eyelash, she refrained from saying. Quit flirting, Mariah!

He ran his fingers along her chin, then tilted her face up until their eyes met. "Dreamier than mine?" he asked in a deep voice.

He's going to kiss me! She sucked in a quick breath.

"I have a confession to make. I might be named after an apostle but I'm no saint. Saints don't covet things that aren't theirs."

Her heart raced. "Are you coveting something or someone?" she asked with a slow bat of her lashes, ignoring every internal warning.

His lips brushed hers, causing warm tremors to flutter down her back. Then the widow's cries filled her mind, causing her body to shake. She scooted back on the bench and breathed deeply, but she choked as the smoky air filled her lungs.

"I'm so sorry, Mariah," Levi said, jumping to his feet. "You have a boyfriend. I shouldn't have tried to kiss you."

And Levi didn't belong to her either, but that didn't stop her from feeling the loss of a man she'd never had. "No. It's not...I don't...How do I say this?"

Levi's phone rang in his pocket. "You don't have to say anything." A look of desperation crossed his face when he stared down at his phone. "I have to take this call. It's from

Africa." He pointed to the front door. "Can you do me a huge favor and if anyone comes into the store, let them know I'll be out in a minute to help them?"

"Sure," she answered, deflated and confused.

He disappeared into the back room, leaving Mariah with a pit in her stomach and a sour taste in her mouth. What had happened to the Montana sunrise and Johnny Nash's sunshiny day?

CHAPTER SIX

*H*e must've misunderstood her. He stepped deeper into the shoe storage room so his voice wouldn't travel outside the gray cinderblock walls. If Mariah overheard their conversation, it would jeopardize everything. He spoke into his phone. "Wait, Mom. Did you say you want me to get her to fall in love with me?"

"Do whatever it takes to keep her there, Levi." His mother's voice held a sense of urgency he didn't hear often. "Spend an exorbitant amount of money on her. It sounds like you care about her. I've never known a girl to *not* fall in love with you. What's the issue?"

"Ha! Like Hannah? I tried for twenty years to get her to fall in love with me and look how that turned out. Now, you expect me to get Mariah to fall in love with me in two hours?"

His mom's long, disappointed sigh carried over the line with clarity. "I'm asking you to be honest with yourself. I know you Levi, and you're not still pining for Hannah. What's going on?"

Only his mother could call him out on something so

sensitive. "You're right. I'm not in love with Hannah, but I want what she and Simon have."

"What?"

"Exactly. What do Hannah and Simon have? What do Nate and Millie have? Until I understand *what* they have, I'll never find the right woman to share my life with. I won't settle for anything less and I'm starting to think that it'll never happen for me."

"Please don't say that."

"You want to know the real reason why I won't be able to get Mariah to stay? She has a boyfriend."

"Boyfriends, girlfriends, fiancés…it's all temporary until you're married."

"I've already tested out that theory with her and got shot down. It's not happening, Mom."

"I'm sorry, Levi." She finally acquiesced. "Tell me everything you know one last time about Mariah. And don't stress about a thing. We'll get a private detective on this. You won't need to do anything else."

"Spy on Mariah? That's worse than trying to get her to fall in love with me. Let me give it another go before Aunt Char sends an investigator to stalk her. Maybe Mariah will give me her contact info and Aunt Char can just call her."

"Wonderful, son. Let me know how it goes. Love you. See you in two weeks. I wish there were a way for us to cut our trip short. Aunt Char is dying to get back, but we still need to deliver the humanitarian packages. Thankfully, she understands the importance of this mission. She's waited this long to meet Mariah; she can wait a few more weeks."

"I thought Dad took you and the Terrences to Africa to go on a safari?"

"Two birds with one stone."

"And Aunt Char is certain Mariah is who she's been looking for?"

"I'm worried what this will do to sweet Charlotte if it's not her. That's another reason I'm encouraging Char not to run to find her just yet. You can help protect Aunt Char's heart, Levi. Find out as much as you can about Mariah. If this girl isn't *her*, then I need to know before Aunt Char does something crazy."

"On it. I left her alone in the store. I'd better get back to her."

"Love you," she said, ending the call before Levi answered her back.

He stared down at his phone and shook his head. He stepped out of the storage room, holding his phone in front of his face. "What if she doesn't want to be found?"

Mariah waved him over to the check-out desk as a family left the store with several shoe boxes. "Who's lost?" she asked with a voice of concern.

He slipped his phone into his pocket. "It's nothing. But did that group just walk out with shoes?" he asked, waving his hand at the window as the family passed. They waved back at him.

"You were taking a really long time, and they were in a hurry to go on a hike, so I sold them a pair of trail runners each. Five in total."

"How?"

"I told them it was all about comfort. They picked the first shoes on the shelves that fit them and asked me how fast I could check them out. I have a degree in finance and your purchasing software is super easy to manipulate. They were in and out of the store in less than ten minutes." She leaned her hip into the desk and placed a hand on top of the computer screen. "But you really should password protect your computer."

"If I told you I was blown away by you, would you believe me?" This woman was smart, kind, and beyond beautiful. She could keep the computer, and the store, if she would just lean against the desk like that and look at him with that same expression of contentment every day. "You're hired. When can you start?"

"Tempting. More than you know, but I just got a call from my friend. He's on his way over right now to pick me up. We need to get on the road."

"You can't go," he said, stepping in front of the door out of desperation. "I still owe you lunch."

"How about the next time I'm in town? Or if you ever make it out to Sacramento?"

There it was! She was at least open to be friends. He played off his relief by running a hand slowly through his hair while he glanced out at the street. He hadn't completely failed his mom and Aunt Char. He stepped away from the door. "I do business in Sacramento, so that'll work. How should I contact you?"

"I signed up for your newsletter promotions. You have my email address. Maybe we can swap Grand Canyon stories." She placed her hand on his arm. "Shoot me an email with some pics after you've hiked it. I'd love to hear your take on the hike. And let me know if you have any fitness pointers for me. I'm trying to get into shape, and I can't think of anyone better to seek advice from," she said, staring at his chest. How could he read that signal wrong? Was she playing with his head?

"Mariah, are you sure you don't have time for lunch, or a cup of coffee?" Three short beeps sounded from the street. Her boyfriend waved to her from his car. "He's not coming in?" Levi didn't even try to mask his irritation.

Mariah's hand flew to her mouth. "Oh no, the bike." She sounded more desperate than he felt. "I need to get that back."

"I already dropped it off this morning."

"And I need to pay for these shoes," she said, pulling a wallet from her purse.

He cupped her hand, then lightly pressed it back into her purse. "Consider it commission." He allowed his fingers to linger, intertwining with hers for a moment in her purse, not wanting to sever the connection. He might as well jeopardize his heart, because this wasn't over for him, even if it was for her. Forget what he wanted, his mom and Aunt Char weren't going to let her go, not yet.

Mariah's violet eyes glistened to a smoky blue, as if she were holding back tears. "Be safe, smokejumper," she said, then reached up and kissed his cheek.

"This isn't goodbye, Strawberry Falls."

"And I hope it never will be," she said, walking away from him.

He stepped out onto the sidewalk and watched Mariah pull away, baffled by what had just transpired between them. He had no option but to go big. His gesture had to be epic. And it couldn't wait.

He whipped out his phone and texted Andy. *I'm coming to your race on Sunday and you're hiking the Grand Canyon with me on Monday. I'll get my contact to reserve us a camping spot near Phantom Ranch. Your shoes need to be comfortable, but most importantly, broken in. I'll bring the rest. See you after the race.*

No way! he texted back.

Levi flipped over the Closed sign, then stepped outside and locked the door. *It's for Mom and Aunt Char. You know why.*

Fine but I'm driving.

Andy was dreaming if he thought Levi would get anywhere near a car with him driving. For some reason Andy thought he could drive inches from other cars while off the racetrack. *No time. Helicopter. But you can hike in our supplies if you want.*

Helicopter.

Levi didn't think he'd be spending another night in the woods so soon, but he knew how to rough it now. Staying at an established campground in tents with access to home-cooked meals would almost be as posh as staying at one of Meri Terrence's oceanside hotels. He laughed at the thought of Meri Terrence spiked out alongside his smelly crew, until the reality of the situation wiped the grin off his face—and who he might have found. Could Mariah be *the* long-lost Terrence girl only spoken of in private whisperings?

CHAPTER SEVEN

a sliver of moonlight pierced through the black forest.

"Please tell me that your car's thermometer is broken," Mariah said, staring at the light on Sebastian's dash that read 20 degrees.

"I wish it were," said Sebastian apologetically, staring straight ahead at the desolate road.

She shivered. "Arizona is synonymous with blistering heat, not blistering cold."

"It won't be cold for long. Once the sun's up," he said, pointing out his window, "the temp should start rising quickly. We're at around 8,300 feet right now. We'll be hiking down to around 2,500 feet where it'll be much warmer, but it still gets cold at night. Good thing we're hiking through and not camping overnight. I'd hate to be one of those poor suckers."

"I hope you're right about us being ready for this," she said with a hint of apprehension.

"It's gonna be rough, no doubt. Your legs will be so tired and sore that you'll want to cry, some people do. Near the end, you'll think you can't walk another foot, but then, miraculously, you'll summit and see the most glorious sunset. Looking down across the canyon, you'll understand what you've accomplished, and all the pain will have been worth it."

"You didn't say anything about serious pain before," she scolded him.

"The pain will pass, but your feeling of accomplishment won't. Knowing you hiked the treacherous twenty-four-mile canyon in one day, you'll feel ready to take on the world." He smacked his palm into his steering wheel. "This'll be so much better than how I'd planned it." Sebastian smiled into the distance as if he'd escaped into another world.

"Planned what?"

He did a double take, like he'd been caught red-handed, then stared back at the road.

"Are we close?" she asked.

"My map app is telling me that we'll be at the trailhead in twenty minutes. We should be starting on the trail by five-thirty. Good thing you got to sleep at 4 pm last night."

"After driving into the early hours yesterday, I'm not so sure twelve hours was sufficient for what we're looking at today." She glared at him. "Considering your little pep talk."

The scowl on her face didn't affect him. "What a great drive. Right? Reminds me of all the good times we've had over the past year."

She wiggled into a more comfortable position and closed her eyes. "The drive's been nice. I'm glad we're doing this." One last road trip to say goodbye to Sebastian. Things would never be the same once they returned to Sacramento. Continuing to hang out with him wouldn't be smart, or kind to either of them.

"There's the sun," he said in a cheery voice. Something had him happy today, which didn't make much sense, considering they'd just broken up. He must really love the Grand Canyon. "Wait. What happened here?"

The forest wasn't only dark with pre-dawn blue mist; it was charred. "Forest fire," she said with a sad moan. Snippets of the firefighter movie played in her mind. Staring at the burnt woods, she envisioned Levi standing waist deep in flames. If she'd been able to Google him, then maybe a burning forest wouldn't be the only thing she'd think when his face popped into her head.

Even though she was not technically Sebastian's girlfriend anymore, she still didn't feel comfortable looking up information about Levi while her recent ex sat next to her in the car.

"Let's check it out," he said, pulling to the side of the road. "It's warmed up to a balmy thirty-five degrees. Want to come out and see the devastation with me?"

"No," she said too quickly, fighting back tears.

"What's wrong?" he asked, cutting the engine.

"I watched a movie the other day about wildfires and how destructive they can be." She glanced out her window. The morning sunlight filtered through the bottom of the trees, casting a shadow across the black ash where bright green had once been. "All I see is death."

"These trees aren't dead, Mariah. Only the underbrush is. I watched a documentary about it too, but in the one I watched, it said that without these fires to clear out the smaller stuff, catastrophic fires occur."

"Those fires are the ones I can't get out of my head," she said, rubbing her temples.

"Come out with me for just a minute. Please. I'll show you what I'm talking about."

She slipped her sweatshirt over her head and opened the door to the arctic. "The cold here is so much worse than in

Idaho because you're not expecting it. This trip has changed my mind about so many things."

"Like what?" Sebastian asked, taking her hand and leading her over to a massive, blackened tree.

The frigid air burned her lungs. "Why did you want me to see this? It makes me feel even worse."

"Look up, Mariah," he said, pointing into the high branches.

Green limbs stretched out from the trunk. Her nerves calmed. "It's still alive? How's that possible? The trunk is completely charred."

"The limbs on these Ponderosa pines grow really high to allow for the fire to pass below. The documentary I saw said that the Ponderosas also grow thick bark that acts as insulation. I'm guessing this tree," he said, pressing his palms into the trunk, "has seen a few fires in its lifetime."

Mariah rested her forehead against the tree. "Why would anyone choose to be a wildland firefighter?" The scent of ash mixed with butterscotch and strawberries filtered out of the tree's bark, warming her senses.

"Good question," said Sebastian. "I have no idea, but I'm sure glad someone's willing to do it to protect these beauties."

"Would you ever consider it?"

"And risk hurting those I care about?" he said, pulling her into an embrace. "Never. I'll always be here for you." His arms were warm and comforting, but she had to stop accepting his succor.

"Sebastian, I really want you to be happy," she said, taking a step back. "Part of that is giving us some distance."

"Is this about your abandonment issues from being adopted? I told you, I'm not going anywhere. I'm not going to die and I'm not going to run off on you."

Her body shook with anger. He'd played the adoption

card again. No matter how many times she told him that she didn't suffer from abandonment issues, he didn't accept it. "That's not what this is about."

"You're shivering," he said, taking her arm. "Let's get you back into the car."

She stomped to the car and plopped into her seat with an audible huff.

He started the engine and turned up the heat, causing the chemical vanilla scent of the car's air freshener to blast her face. He touched her arm. "I'm sorry. I didn't want today to start off like this. I won't say anything else to upset you. Please know that I'm here if you ever want to talk about being adopted and what that means for us," he said, pulling back onto the road.

She bit the inside of her lips closed to keep herself from cussing him out. It was already going to be an incredibly long, arduous day; she didn't want to make it any worse. He'd said he'd play nice; she'd take his word for it and not escalate the situation. After this last expedition with Sebastian, they'd go their separate ways and she'd never have to discuss why her being adopted had nothing to do with the fact that she wasn't in love with him.

"I'm gonna take a quick nap," she said, avoiding his repeated sideways glances.

He wanted to talk, and she had nothing to say that hadn't already been said. She'd known people with the very abandonment issues he was talking about, but that wasn't her. Her last boss had been one of those people, but she was a hoot. Candy MacDonald. The woman sounded like she'd smoked since she was nine. Every morning she'd come into the office and tell Mariah how she'd relaxed on her balcony the night before with a glass of wine in one hand and a cigarette in the other when a bold new idea hit her on how to make the office run smoother. Whatever Candy suggested, they jumped on; the woman knew her stuff. She was *made for the corporate world, not someone to be home mothering*, as she'd put it. Candy's own birth mother had given her up for adoption, so why would she choose to bring any more souls into this world? Mariah's heart broke for Candy every time they spoke about adoption.

Mariah's parents had framed her adoption differently. The thought never crossed her mind of being unwanted. Her birth mother simply couldn't care for her the way she thought someone else would. Yet the security she felt didn't stop her from wondering about the circumstances leading up to her adoption. With her parents' encouragement, she searched out her birth parents...in California...at the adoption agency. Finding out about her birth parents had been the most unsettling day of her life.

The car stopped. "We're here," Sebastian said, jostling her arm. "You awake?"

"I am now," she said, faking a yawn.

Less than five minutes later, they stood in front of the North Kaibab trailhead sign, weighted down with backpacks full of water and salty snacks. They stopped long enough to snap a photo but not read the wall of information.

Mariah's feet pounded the path as they set a brisk 2.5 mile-an-hour pace. With a good half-inch of dust to cushion the trail, she felt like she was gliding down the canyon.

"If we keep up this pace the entire way, maybe a little faster near the bottom, we'll arrive at the top in around twelve hours. Just in time for the sunset," he said with the eyes of a child eyeing a favorite piece of candy.

"What has you in such a good mood this morning?" she asked.

"I'm hiking the Grand Canyon with my favorite person. Do I need any other reason?"

"It's just..." She didn't want to say anything that would

alter his mood, but something was up with him. "You've never been this into hiking before. Your recreation of choice is usually to zip around a seaside town on our bikes, spend the day body boarding, or eating chowder along the wharf."

He shrugged off her comment. "Those are okay, but I have a feeling today is going to be epic. How are your knees? Do you want me to get your poles out?" If Sebastian had always been this accommodating and kind, she might not have broken up with him. He could be so charming at times, but then he'd get something in his head and wouldn't let it go, even if it upset her, like the abandonment conversation earlier. She couldn't get pulled back into a relationship with no future because he decided to be thoughtful one morning.

Ten minutes into their descent, the trail curved, opening to a wide, expansive canyon. The trail snaked along the cliffside before winding along the river at the base of the canyon. "Grand," said Mariah. "John Powell got it right." She paused to take it all in. The soft, red light of the early morning's indirect sunlight caused the jagged red rocks to glow varying shades of sienna and copper. "Golden hour in the Grand Canyon," she said with an unhurried exhale. "Let's get a photo." She dug her phone out of her backpack and snapped a few pics of the scenery, then turned the camera to do a selfie of her and Sebastian. He didn't say a word, simply grinned for the camera. When they restarted their trek, she patted him on his shoulder. "I'm impressed."

"Why?" he asked with a relaxed laugh, his brown eyes glowing amber in the morning light.

"You're not as officious as normal. I thought you'd hit the trail more aggressively, pulling me along with you."

He tilted his face to the sky and breathed in through his nose. "This road trip has made me into new man."

She wrinkled her brow. "You feel like a new man? Why?" He really was in an unusually good mood this morning.

"I think it comes down to acceptance and security. After today," he said with a slow nod and blink, as if she knew what he was talking about, "I have a feeling we'll be filled with both."

Did that mean he'd accepted their break-up and was feeling completely secure with himself? Relief washed over her; grateful their split had been a smooth transition to friendship, as if they'd realized simultaneously that they weren't in love. Her feet had a new spring in them, allowing her to increase her speed. "I like the Grand Canyon on you. You wear it well," she said with a broad smile. "Now, let's get moving."

Sebastian threw his hands in the air. "There's the fire and determination I love. Epic day."

The trail was thick with hikers, mostly around their age, mid to upper twenties. Mariah didn't mind being repeatedly passed by her own cohort and a few teenagers. She and Sebastian stayed in time with the forty-somethings on the trail, leapfrogging each other along the way. Not bad for being out of shape.

Two hours down the canyon, Mariah felt the heat of the day, everywhere, even between her toes. When they'd begun the hike, it seemed unlikely she'd ever warm up. "I need to strip off a layer," she said, removing her backpack while wrestling with her sweatshirt. She kept an eye on her feet and where they traveled as they hit a sharp bend in the trail with a sheer cliff to their left. She felt instant relief from the heat the moment her extra layer was off.

"Here, put it in my backpack. I've got extra room." Sebastian offered, glancing over his shoulder at his backpack. He slowed his pace to a stroll but didn't stop.

"Thanks," she said, unzipping his bag and stuffing her sweatshirt inside.

"Got it?" Sebastian asked while she zipped his backpack

closed. He sped up while she still had a firm grasp on his bag. The movement jerked her forward and to the right. Her body followed the curve of the narrow, cliffside trail.

Her left foot caught on a rock, causing her to break stride and pivot while her torso flew forward. An audible pop echoed off the tall canyon walls. Her left leg gave out and the ground came at her fast. To avoid flying off the cliff, she tucked, throwing her back side against the red rock wall. She crumpled into the ground, her head ultimately resting on a rock. The familiar heat of embarrassment blasted through her body as she quickly pushed herself off the ground.

"Are you okay?" asked a male hiker in a tone that suggested she must be seriously injured after her ugly fall.

She didn't meet the man's eyes, or his companions as they passed her. "Yeah. I'm good. Thanks." She took in a deep breath before taking her first step. When she straightened her left knee, sharp pain shot through it. She'd pulled something. Nothing ibuprofen couldn't fix. Her eyes shot down the trail for Sebastian. By his even stride, he had no idea she'd *fallen behind*; that phrase held an entirely new meaning—one she wouldn't forget any time soon.

Leaning against the rocks for support, she dug into her bag and found her bottle of ibuprofen. She shook four pills out onto her palm and downed them with a long drink of water.

"Mariah!" Sebastian called out, looking a little befuddled.

She waved at him. His eyes grew wide as she limped toward him. "I fell," she said in a strained voice, fighting back the tears.

"Where does it hurt?"

Levi had asked her that same question the last time she'd fallen. If he could see her now, he'd know what an absolute klutz she was. Thankfully, he hadn't been there to see her mortify herself once again. On second thought, if he were there, she'd be in his arms. She'd snuggle her face into his neck while she pressed a hand to his chiseled chest and breathe in his pool water and pine scent.

"Mariah, did you hear me?"

She blinked away the heavenly vision. At least she had a name to go with her perfect dream man now. She may never see Levi Grant again but at least she still had her dreams. "The real question is where *doesn't* it hurt. When this medicine kicks in, the answer will be nowhere."

"Oh good," he said, appeased by her answer. "So, we'll take it slow until the drugs kick in?"

"Yeah, that would be best," she said, hobbling in front of him. "Should I set the pace, then?"

"Set away," he said in a tone of suppressed impatience.

"Sorry to slow us down."

"It's alright. We should still be able to make it by sunset."

Fat chance. With her injury, that was doubtful, but she wasn't about to dash his hopes just yet. Perhaps with the anti-inflammatory drugs in her system, she'd be up to their earlier pace in no time. She focused straight ahead to the south side of the canyon where the path ended on a high precipice. The trail rose to astounding heights, seemingly insurmountable. She retreated to a place in her mind that gave her the willpower to soldier on.

It didn't take long before the sixty-something-year-olds began passing them, kindly offering their own assortment of pain meds. Over the course of the next forty-five minutes, she slowly regained the ability to straighten her knee, experiencing moderate relief from her pain.

"I'm gonna step it up," she said with renewed purpose as they began their trek across a long wooden suspension bridge that crossed over the milky green river below.

"I'm right behind you," Sebastian said in an upbeat voice.

His new positivity helped ease her pain. "If we can regain our earlier pace, we'll reach our oasis in three hours."

"Phantom Ranch? That's where we're stopping to eat lunch, right?" she asked in a hopeful voice. Her mind had been so focused on putting one foot in front of the other, that she hadn't eaten a bite since they'd set out on the trail three hours earlier.

"Yeah, you're going to love their lemonade. But sorry, they don't have corndogs."

"So, you're saying they're not classy," she said, flipping her backpack around and digging out a peanut butter and jelly sandwich. "I can't wait. I'll eat my lunch on the way."

"I like your thinking. That'll allow us to take a shorter break and get back on the trail sooner."

Creamy, salty peanut butter coated the top of her mouth. Peanut butter and jelly had never tasted so good together. "How many more miles before we reach Phantom?"

"Seven. We're halfway there."

"That means we've almost trekked a third of the way by nine o'clock in the morning?"

"Yes, but we've been going downhill. After Phantom, it's all uphill with the afternoon sun beating down on us."

"Lovely," she said, taking the last bite of her sandwich and downing another bottle of water. "Let's do this."

"Show me some fire!" he said with a hoot.

She allowed her laughter to bubble out of her throat. Hopefully, the ibuprofen she'd already taken would be all she'd need to get her through the rest of their hike.

Traversing the river along the snaking switchbacks had her in awe at the canyon's beauty. During the next two hours, little was spoken between them, giving her the opportunity to meditate on the earthly splendor—until her pain returned with heightened discomfort. She couldn't remember when she'd taken her first dose, but it had to have been at least three hours, maybe four.

"How close are we to the ranch?" she asked, reaching her hand into her backpack.

"Just another mile," he said.

She bit down into a green apple. Sour! Her lips puckered, but she continued eating. When she'd taken the first dose of ibuprofen, she hadn't had anything in her stomach, causing mild upset. She wasn't about to make the same mistake twice. "Pain's back. I might need to slow down a bit," she said, crunching another bite of the apple. "Why don't you blaze the trail? I don't mind lagging behind if you want to speed ahead to the ranch and buy our lemonades."

"Really?" he said with more excitement than she'd anticipated. "You don't mind?"

"Not at all." Being alone didn't bother her and she could sense Sebastian's restlessness.

Ten minutes later, she had eight hundred additional milligrams of ibuprofen in her system and Sebastian was out of sight. She breathed in spicy sagebrush and the sweet scent of Cottonwood trees. More than one person congratulated her on hiking the Grand Canyon alone. She simply smiled and thanked them. She had no idea she'd be applauded for walking solo and the men seemed much friendlier. Not only did hiking not require a pricey membership, but she also finally knew where to meet kind, physically minded men. Not that she was in the market; fate had put her on a new course. Now might be the perfect time to take a sabbatical from dating, focus on finding another job, and getting fit. When she'd mastered those two things, she could move on to men. With time, maybe Levi wouldn't seem so perfect to her anymore and she'd find a new perfect someone to crush on who wouldn't leave for a fire assignment and never come home. She'd only thought about him a few times today. With each new day, the warmth of his arms should fade from her memory.

After passing through a thicket of tall grass, she hobbled into a densely wooded area which housed partial civilization. Two-person cabins and picnic tables skirted the river. The trail opened to a large, cleared area with a water filling station and a multi-windowed lodge with the only restaurant along the twenty-three-mile trail. She found Sebastian sitting at a picnic table, tapping an empty plastic cup on the metal surface. The chrome table took her aback; it didn't fit its rustic, natural environment.

"Been waiting long?" she asked, limping to his table.

"About an hour," he said, jumping up and taking her backpack. "Rest while I refill our lemonade."

"An hour?" she asked with surprise. "I had no idea I was that far behind you."

"It's alright," he said, but, by his anxious tone, he hadn't meant it. "When we're together, we'll keep a better pace." He walked toward a line outside a serving window in the lodge.

"I'm not so sure about that," she said to herself. She'd enjoyed the beautiful scenery and her short conversations with fellow hikers while she and Sebastian were separated, but she'd walked as quickly as her injuries would allow. The thought of being pressured by an impatient ex-boyfriend to fight her way up the trail while enduring excruciating physical pain, didn't bring her happy thoughts.

Sebastian returned five minutes later with her lemonade. "Take a sip and tell me this doesn't take the edge off," he said, handing her the lemonade with a smile. He watched her with anticipation as she drank her first gulp.

The drink was yummy, but she was still highly aware of her knee. "That's really good," she said to appease him. "And I think it'll go great with beef jerky. Could you grab mine out of my backpack please?" she asked, dreading the thought of having to walk around the table, then bend her knee to lean down and pick up her pack.

"Sure," he said, handing her a baggie of jerky. He paced back and forth in front of the picnic table for the next ten minutes, his restlessness heightening with every lap.

"That looks so nice," she said, pointing at a couple on the edge of the river with their feet in the water. "My feet have been bugging me. How are your feet?"

Sebastian glanced down at his feet. "Fine. Do you have a second pair of socks? I don't think getting your feet wet is a good idea without a second pair." Now he was just coming up with excuses to get back on the trail. The remainder of the hike was going to be torture if he kept this up, which she knew him well enough to know that this behavior would only intensify until he'd completed whatever task he'd put his mind to.

"I think I need to rest a bit longer," she said, biting into a peppery piece of beef jerky.

He breathed out a sigh and continued pacing.

"Sebastian, were you okay hiking alone? I didn't really mind it."

He perked up. "I could get a head start. Go into the village and check us into our rooms, then order us some dinner." He nodded to himself, strutting around in a circle until he stopped in front of her. "Should I get back on the trail?"

She stared up at the fluffy clouds, as if mulling over *his* suggestion. When she met his questioning eyes, she nearly chuckled at his cute, kid-like hopeful expression. "Only if you think that's best. I'd be totally fine with that."

He didn't waste any time with niceties; he was back on the trail in less than a minute. It also took less than a minute for her fatigue to take hold. She stretched her arms out across the tabletop, then folded them in, resting her head into the inside of her elbow.

CHAPTER EIGHT

*W*hen Mariah woke, the skies were clear, but her head wasn't; it seemed to weigh more. She squinted the afternoon sunlight out of her eyes. At this rate, she'd be hiking up the trail in the dark. At least she'd brought a head lamp, but she needed to get moving. She stood. A knife sliced through her left knee and a thousand needles punctured her feet, or so it felt. She collapsed back into her seated position on the metal bench and wheezed out her discomfort.

Happy voices carried on the wind from the wide, trickling river. If she could just make it to water and soak her feet, she'd be fine…maybe. *I've been through worse,* she told herself, standing again. Although, she couldn't think of a single time in her life where she'd been in more comprehensive physical pain. *One foot in front of the other,* ran through her mind with each excruciating step. Out of her peripheral vision, a man ran toward her.

"Can I give you a hand?" he asked, offering his arm…a tanned, buff arm.

"Levi!" she exclaimed, taking hold of his arm as her knees buckled.

His eyes registered shock. "Mariah, what are you doing here?"

She laughed at his facial expression. "I might ask you the same."

"But you'd told me you were setting up your training to hike the Grand Canyon next year."

"No, I didn't," she said through a grimace of pain. "I said it was my New Year's resolution that I was *setting*. And I set it that day."

"Not sure how setting a *New Year*'s resolution in mid-October works, but here, lean on me," he said, staring down at her feet. "I would've never let you leave the store with a new pair of shoes if I'd known you weren't going to break them in before using them on a hike like this."

Simpleton, she chastised herself. She allowed him to take the brunt of her weight. *Way to reaffirm your lack of intelligence, Mariah.* "I needed to break them in?"

"This is all my fault," he said with a shake of his head. "I should've asked more questions."

"Now *you're* being a simpleton. This has nothing to do with you."

"Hurtful," he said as they reached the water's edge. "And I don't think you're a simpleton."

"After this," she said, motioning to her legs and feet, "you really should. I wasn't prepared for this hike."

"Self-deprecation doesn't suit you," he said, grabbing her arms from the front to help her slowly lower her back side to sit on a log.

"I beg to disagree. We should never take ourselves too seriously."

He kneeled in front of her and untied her laces. "I agree with you there."

She raised an eyebrow. "We finally agree on something."

He pulled off her shoe to a blood-soaked, white sock. Fear crossed his face. "Mariah, how long have your feet been hurting?"

Her stomach turned as he peeled off her sock to uncover several open sores, blisters which had popped, then been rubbed raw. "Not until I stopped. I don't understand."

"That concerns me," he said, placing her foot in the freezing stream water. "Are you diabetic?"

The water stung but eased the pain. "No. I've never been…" her voice faded as she tried to think of what the symptoms of diabetes were.

"Have you ever lost feeling in your feet before?"

"Not that I can remember. I felt them this morning. Less than an hour into the hike, they felt hot between my toes."

Anger flashed across his face. "You had hot spots and you didn't take care of them?"

She shook a finger in the air. "Now, if I'd ever heard of these so-called *hot spots*, then I would've. I was too preoccupied with simply walking after I fell and injured my knee." *Dang!* She wasn't going to mention her fall.

"You hurt your knee? How badly?" he said, looking from knee to knee. He sighed. "Your left knee is swollen."

"It's okay," she said, trying to talk him off whatever ledge he found himself on because of *her* injuries. "I've been taking ibuprofen since around nine o'clock. I'm fine."

He cocked his head to the side. "How much ibuprofen have you taken?"

"Eight."

He coughed. "You've taken 1600 milligrams in less than five hours?"

"When you say it that way, it sounds like a lot."

"No wonder you didn't feel your blistering feet," he said,

removing her other shoe and sock to find the same grotesque sores. "And next time, don't wear cotton socks."

"What should I—"

"Anything," he said in an angry tone, cutting her off. "Anything but cotton. Didn't you ever hike in Strawberry Falls?"

"Of course, but for an hour or two, not twelve to fifteen hours, traversing the most epic canyon in the world." She sounded like Sebastian. Her spirits dipped, thinking how upset Sebastian was going to be when she reached the top at midnight. With her injuries, she'd be lucky to keep even a slow pace of one mile an hour.

Levi raised his eyes to hers. They held a new level of sympathy. "Sorry. I didn't mean to be so hard on you. Let me get a good look at your knee," he said, gently pinching her leggings and pulling them up to above her knee. "I need to feel both knees to understand any irregularities in your left knee. Do you see how it's swollen?" He asked running his hand down her thigh and cupping her knee.

His touch sent a heat wave up her sides and into her chest. "Sorry, what was that?"

He did the same thing on her other leg. "Do you see the difference? How your left knee is puffy with fluid, and your right knee isn't."

She had no idea what he was talking about and didn't care. Staring at his moving lips was all that mattered. "Yeah. Is that bad?" Nothing felt bad when Levi touched her.

"Could be. What happened?"

"I was grabbing onto Sebastian's backpack, then I tripped and twisted my knee. It went out and I fell, hitting my head."

"Wait, you didn't hit your knee?" he asked, doing a double take on her hairline by her left ear. "You have a little blood here." He wiped the side of her face with a wet cloth. "Where's Sebastian?"

"He went on ahead."

"He *what?*" Levi yelled.

Her feet were nearly frozen. "You don't happen to have a towel, do you?" she asked, lifting her feet out of the water.

"Hold tight," he said, jogging away. He bolted across a bridge that led to a campsite area. He hadn't told her that he was hiking the Grand Canyon this week, had he? She didn't remember that being part of their conversation. He returned five minutes later with a huge backpack in a sunken state, looking as if its contents had recently been removed.

"Did you tell me you were hiking the Grand Canyon this week?"

"No. I decided on Saturday to come," he said, pulling a gray hand towel out of his bag.

"You're more spontaneous than me," she laughed out.

He patted her left foot with the towel, causing her wounds to sting. Her body tensed. She took in a long breath to calm her frazzled nerves.

"Is that a good thing?" he asked.

"Very good," she said, tilting her head to the side and watching him intently as he smoothed antibacterial cream between her toes. She giggled. "That tickles."

"Sorry," he said, intonating he was more pleased with himself than sorry. "Better to tickle than hurt."

"Have to agree with you on that one. How are your feet?"

"Good. I'm used to hiking long distances."

"I'm floored you decided to come down here last minute."

He stroked the side of her foot with one hand as he applied a fuzzy bandage to her sores with the other. "You inspired me."

No one had ever told her that she'd inspired them before. She cooed inside. "I'm the reason you're here?"

He slipped a new sock onto her foot, then moved his attention to her other foot. As he held her foot in his hand, he zoned out, staring across the river. She wiggled her toes, causing him to blink. "Yes." He looked at her as if he wanted to ask her something, then bowed his head and continued caring for her foot.

"Thank you. I know you don't think you're my guardian angel, but how do you explain us running into each other like this? You being here at the exact moment I needed you?"

"Stalking," said Andy, walking up to them. "That's one way to explain it."

"Andy!" She clapped her hands, then held them together at her chest. "I didn't know you were here."

"That's because *I'm* not the one stalking you," he said with a playful wink.

She rubbed Levi's arm. "Levi can stalk me all he wants as long as he brings his first aid kit along with him."

"That looks painful," said Andy, motioning to her foot.

"Not as painful as my knee," she said.

The men furrowed their brows while they focused on her knee.

"What happened?" asked Andy.

"It's really not a big deal. My leg twisted, my knee popped, then I went down."

Levi stopped bandaging her foot. "Did you say that your knee popped when you pivoted?"

"Then it gave out?" asked Andy.

By the concerned look on their faces, whatever she'd said had them worried. "Is that disconcerting?" she asked, hoping they'd say no.

"Maybe," said Levi. "Can I take another look at your knee? You should have an orthopedic surgeon do this, but since we're out in the middle of nowhere, let's see what we can determine. I've been to enough of Nate's doctors' appointments with him to know a little. He's had every type of knee injury you could imagine."

She swallowed down her fear. "Alright," she said in agreement.

Levi turned to his brother. "Can you help me get her to the picnic table? I want to set her on top where it will be easier to assess her knee."

He needs help getting me up onto a picnic table? Dang! Why did I have to wear form-fitting clothes again? Her body image insecurities rose to the surface while they each took an arm and leg and lifted her up the small hill and onto the picnic table. She crossed her arms over her tummy as it popped up above her leggings in her seated position.

Levi placed his knee under her left thigh. "This will help stabilize your knee." He then moved her kneecap back and forth. "Does that hurt?"

She felt a slight tug but not much pain. "Not really."

He held her ankle and tapped her calf on the underside of her leg with his fist. "I want you to think about how this feels and if it's the same or different when I tap your other leg." He moved to the other side of the table and did the same exercise on her right leg.

Her right leg had a springy feeling the left hadn't. "Mountain bike versus beach cruiser," she said, scared of what he was about to tell her.

"That's a great analogy." His voice held a tone of surprise and admiration. "Your right leg has elasticity because of your ACL. It's a ligament that helps stabilize your knee joint. It connects your thigh bone to your shin bone and allows you to perform a pivoting motion. Your left leg doesn't have that same plasticity. I think you snapped your ACL when you stopped suddenly and pivoted—when you heard the popping sound.

She bit her lip and grimaced. "That sounds bad."

Levi placed his hand lightly on her shoulder. "Look on the bright side. With surgery, you'll be as good as new, maybe even better because you'll have a stronger ligament in there. And…" he said as if he were announcing a grand prize winner, "you might even get a helicopter ride out of it."

She narrowed her eyes. "Helicopter ride?"

"Out of here. Before the sun sets. You can't hike on that leg," he said, pointing to her left leg. "And you need a doctor to examine that knee."

Failure, ran through her mind. She'd be a big fat failure if she stopped now. "Isn't the slogan for the Grand Canyon, down is optional, up is mandatory?"

Levi's face hardened with determination—the same look she'd imagined him having while he sprinted into a forest fire. "You're injured. Either I talk to mountain rescue and they haul you out of here or I arrange for a helicopter to take you out."

"Helicopter? You can do that?"

"If you're injured, yes. I know people."

"I've come this far," she said with a defiant shake of her head. "I'm not being flown out of here. I'm finishing this."

He cocked an eyebrow. "Why are you being so stubborn?"

"You call this stubborn? You really don't know me. Do you?"

"You can't say I'm not trying." He pushed his hair back through his fingers while he paced in a circle. "Give me one good reason to let you walk out of here," he said through gritted teeth.

"I'll give you three," she said, shooting daggers from her eyes at him. "One, I can't afford a helicopter extraction. I got laid off last week. I don't have insurance and I can't afford to see a doctor. Two, I'm not giving up. I've made it this far. I'm mentally tough. I can do this." She rubbed her chin in thought. "And three, you can't make me."

"That's mature of you, Strawberry Falls." Levi looked to Andy for help.

Andy simply shrugged and said, "You're the one stalking her. Don't look at me."

Fate could very well be laughing at her again, or someone in heaven protected her. Stalking had nothing to do with them running into each other again. She'd known the stalking type, and Levi was no stalker.

"And I'm not about to stop now." Levi's left eye twitched. "If you insist on making this hard on everyone, so be it, but you're spending the night in my tent."

Did he say in *his* tent? Her body broke out in a sticky sweat.

Levi pointed at his brother. "Andy, are you okay hiking out this afternoon? Someone needs to tell Mariah's friend that she's with me now. *I'll* make sure she makes it out safely tomorrow." His nostrils flared. "It may take us all day."

She wasn't about to be the recipient of anyone's pity, especially Levi's. She twisted her torso and stretched her arm to grab her backpack from the far end of the table, then slid it onto her lap. She slowly swung her legs down and set her feet onto the bench in preparation to step off the picnic table and start back on the trail. "Levi, I appreciate your concern. I understand you're upset with my decision to finish this hike, but I'm not asking you to help me. If I start back on the trail right now, it might take me several additional hours to reach the top but walking in the dark doesn't bother me in the slightest. No big deal."

Levi's fists clenched at his sides. "It *is* a big deal," he countered, pointing to the trail where it wound up the side of the cliff. "In your condition and without a light, you could walk yourself right off the cliff, and you need to rest. You need to rest your bloody feet, rest your knee, and…well…rest everything." By the look of determination in his eyes, he wasn't backing down either. He'd held his head high while he spoke his mind. The fire in his eyes told her he was a man who'd been raised to act according to his own conscience, no matter the personal sacrifice. Her admiration for him only heightened, while anger boiled in her gut at his sympathy.

She met his stare with the same level of intensity. "I won't be your charity case, Levi."

He sat on the metal bench below her, his arms brushing her legs. "Please let me do this for you, Mariah. I hadn't meant to sound so upset. It just frustrates me that your boyfriend left you alone to fend for yourself. Why are you with that guy anyway?"

His protectiveness had her smiling inside. "I'm not," she said calmly.

"I know. He's not here," he said, wringing his hands. "I mean, why are you dating him? You should be with someone who doesn't run off on you like that when you need him."

"I'm *not* with him. I was the one who suggested he go on ahead because he was starting to get on my nerves, in a big way."

Levi's eyes brightened. "You broke up?"

"During my birthday dinner. I knew that day that..." *I would never bat my lashes at him like I do at you,* "we didn't have a future together."

Andy stepped in front of them. "And that's my cue to leave. Please listen to Levi, Mariah," he said, glancing at his brother. "I hate to admit this but he's the expert here. He'll keep you safe. And hey, maybe you crazy kids will have a good time after all. Enjoy your charred marshmallows over the campfire while I'm enjoying a steak dinner."

Mariah's stomach gurgled. "With how hungry I am, I'd take burnt marshmallows or even those slimy French snails right about now," she said with a laugh, then realized by their serious facial expressions that the snails were a delicacy and she'd dissed their family's restaurant. Her hand flew to her mouth. "I'm so sorry. Your family is exquisite." The brothers' faces both raised into the same amused smile. When she realized she'd allowed a Freudian slip to pass her lips, she hurriedly said, "Your family's restaurant is exquisite."

Andy grabbed hold of his brother's shoulder. "Not as exquisite as this man," he said, looking between them. "I'll be thinking of you two when I'm eating my steak," he said, glancing back at them as he walked away.

"I know I dissed his snails, but that was low," Mariah said with narrowed eyes.

"Little does he know that I ordered us steak dinners here at the lodge tonight."

"I don't care what you say, you're my angel," she said, leaning over and wrapping her arms around his shoulders and chest. She rested her head on his shoulder with her cheek rubbing against his neck. Her eyelids grew heavy. She would've dozed off to sleep if she hadn't been so hungry.

"Dinner isn't for another hour, but I'll find you something else to eat," he said, patting her arm as if he'd expected her to release him, but her comfort level was somewhere between glorious contentment and transcendental satisfaction.

She relaxed to the steady rhythm of her own heartbeat. "I'm good for a few minutes. This is really comfortable."

"I have a better idea. Let me carry you to my tent."

Her eyes flew open as she threw herself back. "I didn't mean it like that."

He scratched the back of his head. "Judging by your reaction, neither did I. It might've sounded like I'm trying to benefit from your injury. I'm not."

"I believe you," she said with a tired smile.

"You could use some rest. My tent is now yours. I'm used to sleeping under the stars. I actually prefer it."

She must've made him feel the need to explain himself. "I feel silly for insinuating that—"

"Don't be. Your innocence is refreshing," he said,

standing. "Can I carry you to the tent? You should lie down and elevate your knee. I'll give you some Tylenol. No more ibuprofen for the evening."

She opened her arms. "I'm all yours." And there she was again, unable to control her flirting. Being in his presence made her do and say crazy things. She knew her heart would hate her later, but she couldn't seem to stop herself from swooning in Levi's arms.

"Careful what you say," he said, scooping her up. "I might just take you up on your offer."

She melted into him like coconut salve being rubbed into his strong, tanned shoulders on a hot day at the beach—the nutty-scented oil dripping down his strong back. She cleared her throat. There she was again, fantasizing over a man she couldn't and shouldn't have. The vision in her mind of a hot day at the beach changed to a burning forest. Shivers cascaded down her spine. "Do you ever get scared?" she asked as he set her onto a sleeping bag in a mustard-colored tent. The tent smelled like her high school gymnasium during a wrestling match, a mixture of men's stale sweat and a synthetic wrestling mat.

"Only on Halloween when I'm forced to eat candy corn."

"What?" she laughed out. "Where did that come from?"

He stuffed a pillow under her left knee, propping it up. "Isn't everyone terrified of candy corn? It's horrible in every way."

"Well, I guess that's it then. We're over, you and me, because I happen to like candy corn. At least I like the top section that's white. I bite off the white, then throw away the rest."

"Ha!" he yelled out, squeezing an instant cold pack in his hands. "Exactly my point. If you had to eat the entire thing, you'd gag and never eat them again."

She pinched her chin between her forefinger and thumb. "Am I sensing childhood trauma here?"

"Yes, doctor. Can you help me? I think I suffer from caramelaphobia," he said with a chuckle, applying the cold pack to her knee.

She pointed at him. "That's *not* a real condition."

"I swear it is. Look it up."

She pulled her phone from her pocket and tapped on her Google app, but the screen displayed no service. "You got me," she said, lowering her torso down until her head rested comfortably against the pillow. "Do you always hike with plush, down pillows? Not that I'm complaining, mind you."

"That's Andy's pillow. He has richer tastes than I do these days. That wasn't always the case."

"You mean when you were a hot-shot lawyer living in LA and had lots of money?"

His eyes lowered. "Not exactly." He drew out the last word as if she were getting close to discovering who he was but didn't have him pegged quite yet.

"Please don't take what I'm saying the wrong way because I think I get where you're coming from. I love the city life on *weekdays*. I chose employment where I'd make okay money but nowhere near the cash I would've made if I'd chosen to take a position with a big accounting firm. Having my evenings and my weekends off to relax with friends at a trendy restaurant or on the beach is my idea of the quintessential life. Until last week, I was living that dream."

He ran his hand down her arm in a comforting way. "I'm sorry you lost your job, but fate may have stepped in, throwing you on a new course of adventure and momentary gain." He rummaged through a second huge backpack that would have swallowed her whole, and pulled out a baggie filled with freeze-dried, sliced strawberries and bananas.

"Here it is," he said, handing her the baggie. "These beauties will make the world feel right again."

She wrinkled her nose. "You think I should invest in freeze-dried fruit?" she said, confused by his statement.

"Ah? No. Those are to replenish your electrolytes. The adventure and monetary gain will happen when you come work for me."

"You want me to work at the running store?" she said, chomping down a few strawberries. He was right. No sooner had she started eating the crunchy, tangy fruit and her energy spiked. Why hadn't she thought to bring freeze-dried fruit on the hike?

He nodded, causing a zing of excitement to pulse through her until the irony of her current situation slapped her in the face.

"But I don't run. When I try to *walk*, this is what happens," she said, pointing at her knee. "No one will want to buy running shoes from me."

He puffed air out the side of his mouth. "You already did, and I said you were hired. Remember? So, it's all legit. I can retro your start date and offer you health insurance. Your knee will be covered, and you'll have income to get you back on your feet." He tapped his chin while he stared up at the corner of the tent. "I've been thinking about transferring to a smokejumper camp outside of Sacramento. I have a few buddies on that crew who I went through training with. You could run a store for me there in Sacramento if you want to stay in the area."

Her mouth dropped open. "Did you decide to open a store in Sacramento within the past thirty seconds?" she asked with renewed admiration.

His blue eyes sparkled with purpose. "I've never had a difficult time making or executing decisions. Sometimes I make the wrong decision, but you'll find that I don't dawdle on an idea."

"I believe that," she said, contemplating his offer. "You're the most courageous person I've ever met. It takes guts and determination to start a business." If she worked for him, spent time with him every day, she'd fall in love with him for sure. She was half in love with him already. But how could she say no? With her knee injury, she needed health insurance—desperately. "Can I think about it?"

"Take your time," he said, opening a cookie tin containing an assortment of nuts, dark chocolates, and hard cheese cubes.

She wiggled her brow. "Is this bribery?" she asked, taking a handful of his deluxe snacks. "Because I'm down with bribes." She popped a piece of chocolate into her mouth and moaned as cinnamon chocolate with a hint of turmeric melted into her tongue. "You've got to be kidding me," she said with a smile of contentment while she bit into a cheese chunk, savoring how the creamy and salty sweet flavors blended together to bring out each other's unique flavors. "I thought you said you didn't have rich tastes? Where did you come up with the idea of pairing gourmet cheeses with expensive chocolates?"

His facial expression grew cautious, as if she'd uncovered one of his secrets. "I don't know. It's something we sell at the Mandolin," he said with ease, snapping back to his normal, carefree demeanor. "How's your pain level?"

She'd almost forgotten why she was in his tent in the first place. "In this position, with the cold pack, it doesn't hurt at all. I can't thank you enough."

He released a sigh of relief. "We'll hold off on the Tylenol until you're ready to go to sleep. Considering your day, how would you feel about hitting the hay around six, at sundown?"

She rubbed her eyes and yawned. "What time is it now?"

"It's close to four."

"I'll try, but with you making me so comfortable, I'm not sure I can stay awake for two more hours. A story might help. Tell me about Sun Valley."

"Okay, but I want to hear all about growing up in Strawberry Falls."

"Boring. Are you sure you don't want to hear about Sacramento?"

"I'm sure. Our childhood experiences mold us, sometimes more than our own genes. I'd love to hear about your parents and how your family ended up in Strawberry."

Mariah floated in and out of sleep while Levi theatrically related childhood adventures with his brothers until the light outside the tent faded to dark blue. She wasn't sure if she believed his fishing stories. Didn't all men have legendary fishing tales? The lodge staff delivered their meals to the tent. Tent-side service while camping? Levi had a way of making friends, friends who catered to him.

"How did you like your steak?" Levi asked, taking her empty plate.

"I seriously think that was the best meal I've ever eaten."

He chuckled. "Food's always better after a long hike. Here," he said, handing her two acetaminophen tablets. "Hopefully, this'll control the pain tonight."

"I'm not sure I need it. If I don't move my leg, then it doesn't hurt."

"That's a relief, but you need it. We don't want your pain to sneak up on us. Besides your knee, your thigh muscles are most likely going to experience the 'pains of success' tomorrow."

"No pain, no gain?"

"The Grand Canyon is the literal embodiment of that

statement. I've never known anyone to *not* feel leg muscle aches after hiking the Grand Canyon. Not one."

She raised a brow. "Even the mighty smokejumper himself, who's used to hikes like this?" She teased him.

"Why do you think I decided to break up the hike into two days? I like to spread out my pain, unlike someone else I know," he said, playfully patting her thigh. Mariah shivered. He retracted his hand. "Sorry. I didn't mean—"

"No, it's not that. My thigh muscles could actually use a good massage," she said, rubbing her arms to combat the chill. "It's getting cold."

"Yeah. It might be chilly tonight. Do you need to use the restroom before I help you into your sleeping bag?" he said, unzipping a sleeping bag, splaying it open, then spreading it out next to her.

She twisted her lips in thought. "No, which is odd, because I can't remember the last time I used the bathroom."

His face registered concern. "I'll make sure you drink more tomorrow. For now, I'm going to lift you slightly off the ground and reposition you onto this bag, okay?"

"That's a lot of work," she said, pressing her palms into the ground and pushing herself up. She scooted over until she was on top of the open sleeping bag. "I got this."

"You're one tough cookie," he said with a look of wonder.

"Thanks for the compliment. I consider myself reasonably tough if weather isn't a factor. I'm what you call a fair-weather enthusiast. Would you stay with me tonight to keep me warm?" His eyes went wide. "For more body heat in the tent." She quickly clarified, then held her breath, awaiting his response.

"I don't know how I feel about that," he said, making himself comfortable on the other sleeping bag. By his actions, he'd agreed to stay inside the tent with her. "You sure that's what *you* want?"

She'd play along with his little game. "That depends. Do you snore?"

He snapped, then shot her a finger gun. "Spoken like a true snorer. I was going to ask you that same question before agreeing to sleep with you."

Heat flowed up her neck and into her cheeks. She crossed her arms over her chest. "Watch your tongue."

"Didn't like the snore comment?" he asked with a hint of a laugh. "That may have been too edgy and presumptive of me. I apologize if I offended you."

"Nice concession," she said sarcastically, pulling the sleeping bag over her shoulder while wiggling into a comfortable position on her side to face him. She couldn't get enough of their bantering, but her eyelids, along with every muscle in her body, told her she'd be asleep in a few minutes, whether she liked it or not. She yawned. "Good night, smokejumper."

"Sweet dreams, Strawberry Falls," he said in almost a whisper.

Her eyes remained focused on his beautiful face for as long as she could keep them open. Luckily, she'd memorized his strong jawline, his perfect lips, and his clear blue eyes. She dozed off to sleep with him at her side...

They walked along the same trail she'd hiked earlier in the day, passing over the foamy green river. She squeezed Levi's hand. "Come find me," she said playfully, before running off the trail into the thickest section of the forest, dense with cottonwood trees, their bright yellow leaves at the peak of change. She pushed aside crisp red underbrush as she wove her way toward higher ground.

Heavy footsteps grew increasingly closer as Levi closed the gap between them. With every crunch of his steps, a thrill of excitement sped her heart.

"Mariah, I have to go. Don't follow me," he said in a voice of caution.

"What?" she asked over the roar of a freight train. She turned in a circle, frantically listening for his footsteps but they were drowned out by the noise of a...her heart stopped when she noticed the flames, less than a football field up the steep red wall. Two teenagers waved their arms in the air as the flames approached them from below. Black smoke clouded her vision. Levi wouldn't make it to the teenagers. She had to stop him. She ran toward the smoke. Her knee screamed in pain as she fell to the ground. Lying on her side, Mariah looked around. A walking stick rested near her head. With the help of the stick as a crutch, she painfully rose to her feet, then hobbled swiftly up the hill, following the freshly charred landscape.

She stood in the same black forest she'd been in before she'd begun the hike. Only now, Levi laid at her feet on his back. Smoke rose from his body. She tried to kneel at his side, but the pain in her knee was too acute so she laid at his side. The breath of life had left his body, leaving him quiet and still. She drew in a sharp breath and collapsed onto his chest. She cried out in agony while she pressed her lips to his. They were still warm. Hope stirred inside her. Maybe he still had a chance. "Don't leave me," she petitioned both him and heaven above. "Please, don't leave me. I need you." She kissed him again and again, until he started to stir.

CHAPTER NINE

*R*ain pelted Levi's face, pulling him out of his deep slumber and into a blurry, half-awakened state. His eyes were too heavy to open but he was alert enough to know he should listen for thunder. Rain meant lightning and lightning meant fire.

"Don't leave me." Mariah's panicked voice rang above his head as if her body floated within the rain cloud. It wasn't unusual for him to dream about saving beautiful women in distress, but this dream was different. "Please, don't leave me. I need you." Mariah dropped out of the sky and landed on top of him. Her torso pressed against his chest. Her soft wet lips made him want to cry out his desire for her, but she was the one crying. Her tears had been showering his face, not rain.

The air in the tent grew heavy. He woke to Mariah kissing him with an elemental passion he'd never experienced before, causing his body to shift into overdrive. She stopped just long enough to beg him to stay, then kissed him again. "Mariah," he said, cupping her moist face. Her eyes focused on his lips. "What's wrong?"

Relaxation sighed through her body. With a whisper on her breath, she rolled onto her side.

"Mariah," he called to her, but she didn't rouse. She'd fallen asleep again. Or she'd never awoken. Had she been dreaming while she kissed him? He wracked his brain, trying to remember if she'd called out his name. He longed to wrap his arms around her waist and have her beg him, again and again, to stay. In her dream, was he the man she was begging to stay? He laid on his back and stared at the tent's low ceiling. One thing was for certain, he couldn't stay another minute in the tent, or he might wake Mariah with his own fiery kisses.

The early morning temps chilled Levi's bones but welcomed him with a sky of glistening stars. He set his sleeping bag next to the tent and slipped inside with a frustrated grunt.

"Bummer, man," said a fellow camper, walking by on the path next to the tent which led to the restrooms. The man's deep voice didn't match his small stature. "We've all been there."

It took Levi a few seconds to understand the guy's meaning. He thought Levi had been thrown out of the tent after a lovers' quarrel. "It's not that," Levi said as if he needed to save face with the stranger. "More like the opposite."

"Then what are you doing out here?" the guy scoffed.

I'm an idiot! Levi chastised himself. *I can't allow this moment to pass.* Mariah had asked him to stay with her, then kissed him. She'd beckoned *him*. Levi jumped out of his sleeping bag and unzipped the tent. He sped to her on his hands and knees, ultimately leaning over her in preparation to wake her with *his* kisses. Moonlight shone in through the tent's opening, causing Mariah's face to glow. She radiated innocence and goodness. He stared at her, dumbstruck by her natural beauty. He thought of her scared plea for him to stay. A fierce need to protect her burned inside him, overpowering all other desires. Lowering himself down with his arms in a pushup, he kissed her forehead, promising to protect her for as long as she allowed him to.

Levi had no idea how long he'd stared into Mariah's face before he found himself back outside in his sleeping bag, staring up at the silent stars. Sunlight blushed the horizon, causing the stars to lose their brilliance. Contentment filled his breast. He exhaled, slow and long. His breath froze, suspended in the air over his head like a steam cloud.

"Levi?" Mariah called to him.

"Here," he said, climbing into the tent to find her sitting up with a sleepy smile on her face.

"Did you spend the night out in the cold?" she asked, wrinkling her forehead.

Guilt settled in his gut. He'd told her he'd stay with her in the tent. He'd abandoned his post. He couldn't explain to her how he didn't trust himself to sleep next to her after she'd kissed him, nearly driving him mad with desire to kiss her back. He had to come up with something to explain why he'd left her. "I heard a noise and thought I'd protect you from the wild cats."

Her left brow shot up. "Like the dangerous wild animals in Sun Valley?" she said with heavy sarcasm.

By her reaction, she knew he was lying. "Exactly. I may have laid it on a bit thick the other day, but this is no joke. Where there are elk and deer, there are mountain lions. Lion sightings happen almost daily in my valley."

"And are there elk and deer in the Grand Canyon?"

"Yes. And do you want to know who the largest predators are?"

She giggled in her throat as she wiggled out of her sleeping bag. She seemed to favor her good leg, but her pain level didn't appear to be anywhere near where it had been yesterday afternoon when he'd found her near the river. Asking about her pain might call her attention to her injuries so he ignored it the same way she did.

"No," she said in a teasing tone.

He shouldn't have cried wolf about the wild cats the other night because now she wasn't taking him seriously. "I'm going to tell you anyways. Mountain lions. Although attacks on humans are rare, it happens. We lose dogs to cougars all the time in the Ketchum area. You can't be too careful."

"With less than two dozen fatal cougar killings in the past hundred years, I'll take my chances," she said, tying her shoelaces. "Should we break camp and get on the trail?"

He leaned to his side as she moved past him toward the tent opening. "How do you know that?"

"After you scared me the other night, I researched the probability of getting attacked by a *wild cat*," she said, stepping out of the tent. Sunshine danced on her face as she stretched her back and walked in a circle, testing out her left leg.

"How did you sleep?" he asked, motioning to her leg, but hoping she'd bring up the fact that she'd kissed him.

"Good. Have you ever experienced a nightmare that transformed into the most rewarding dream ever?" Her eyes sparkled with glee.

Thank you, heaven above! shouted though his mind. "Boys have those dreams all the time."

Her eyes widened in shock, or possibly disgust.

Levi didn't wait a second to explain. "I'm talking about the dream where earth has been invaded by aliens and I'm the only capable person who ends up saving the world, or the dream where a beautiful woman is attacked by a mountain lion and I fend off the beast with my bare hands." He shot an arm in the air triumphantly.

"Oh," she said, eyeing the bathroom. "You do understand.

I'll be right back." She walked quickly away from him, hobbling slightly, but nothing like yesterday where she'd needed to be carried. How could she leave him like that without explaining her dream to him?

Levi had the tent down and the backpacks packed in less than five minutes.

The young park ranger he'd chatted with yesterday walked up to him. "Hey, Levi. You still got those extra shoes you mentioned?"

Levi's eyes went to the guy's vest. "Yeah, *Mike*," he said, pulling his extra trail runners from his pack and setting them onto the picnic table.

Mike sighed out his relief. "Would you mind seeing if they fit an inexperienced hiker? His feet are a mess. He wore brand new hiking shoes, like your friend, but his boots are two sizes too small for his feet."

"No problem. Bring him over and we'll try these babies out on him."

Mike gripped the rim of his iconic, National Parks, broad-brimmed straw hat and tipped it. "I'll hook you two up with breakfast."

"That'd be great," Levi said with sincere appreciation. Park rangers ate well. He and Mariah would be fed and on the trail by seven o'clock at this rate. "Not a bad way to start the day," he said aloud to himself.

"What's not a bad way to start the day?" Mariah asked. She wore a bright red, lightweight shell jacket that caused her eyes to change from periwinkle to deep purple.

He swallowed to combat his instant dry mouth, reminding himself to breathe. When he caught his breath, he said, "A day that begins with you, of course."

Her lavender eyes brightened. "What are you selling today?" she said in a playful voice until she noticed their tent was down. She pointed to their campsite. "You've already broken camp?" Her face dropped with disappointment.

"You like camping? I thought you were more of a city girl?"

"Why do you keep saying that?" she asked with a tsk of her tongue. "I love city life, but that doesn't mean I don't like nature and camping."

He rubbed his chin. "Fishing?"

"Absolutely. If I don't have to slice open a live fish, I'll be right there at your side in the boat."

"Really?" he asked with more enthusiasm than he'd meant to give. So much for playing it cool to appear only moderately interested in her. "You'll be beside me?"

"Yeah, I'll be in the boat with the other fish you've already reeled in."

His heart skipped a beat before pumping increased blood through his veins. Was that an invitation or had he read her wrong again? "I'm sorry. What?"

Her gaze dipped to the ground while her cheeks blushed bright pink. She raised her eyes slowly, her lashes fluttering until their eyes met again.

Time to charm! No holding back now. Mariah didn't have a boyfriend and he was going to make sure that he was the top contender for the position.

Mike walked toward them, carrying two plates loaded with scrambled eggs, sausage patties, and biscuits laden with thick gravy. "Breakfast *for* champions," he said, placing the plates on the picnic table in front of Mariah.

Mariah picked up her fork. "Remind me to camp with you more often. Seriously, though," she said, pointing her fork at Mike. "How does Levi get first-class treatment while *camping* in a national forest?"

Mike smacked Levi's shoulder. "Firefighter. Smokejumper. Grant philanthropist. You're hanging with one of the best of us. Watch," he instructed her, waving over a teenager.

Although Levi appreciated Mike's praise, he didn't deserve it. "Mike, you're exaggerating," he said with a shake of his head.

The thin, timid boy stumbled over to them, wincing with every step.

"Ouch," said Mariah. "Is that how I looked yesterday?"

"No," said Levi. "You looked ten times worse. Aren't you glad you rested for the night?"

She ran her fingers through her hair. "More than you'll ever know."

Levi did a double take. He hated to pull his eyes from Mariah but forced himself to focus on the teenage boy as he sat opposite Mariah on the picnic table. "What's your name?"

The boy scowled as he untied his hiking boots. "Scotty."

"Are your parents Star Trek nerds?" Levi asked, scratching the fresh stubble on his chin.

The boy rolled his eyes. "No. They *are* Scottish. So much worse."

Levi laughed. "I'm the one trying to take your mind off this," he said, yanking the first boot from the boy's foot.

Scotty howled out in pain, then nearly hyperventilated.

"Wait!" shouted Mariah, running around the table as if her feet and knee weren't bothering her. She sat next to Scotty and took his hand in hers, placing it in her lap. "Look into my eyes and squeeze my hand as hard as you can." She instructed him.

One look into Mariah's caring violet eyes was all it took for Scotty to become a complete vegetable. "Are those real?" he asked.

Levi took the opportunity to pull the other boot off.

Mariah smiled. "I'm assuming you mean my eyes. Yes, they're as natural as rain on a sunny day."

Scotty squirmed slightly when Levi removed his socks and began applying the antibacterial ointment to his sores. "Does it ever rain when it's sunny?"

"Yes," answered Mariah. "But it's rare, like my eyes. My mom told me that she'd never known anyone else to have eyes the same color as mine. She said that when God wanted to mark something special, he sent rain on a sunny day. When I was born, it rained but the sun also shined bright through a thin cloud, sending her a sign that I was meant to be hers."

Levi froze. Should he tell her now who he thought she was? Who everyone in his family hoped she would turn out to be? Mike bumped his leg into Levi's side, waking him from his trance. Levi blinked a few times before continuing to bandage up Scotty's feet. "The shoes I have should fit you." Scotty waved a hand at Levi as if he were listening, but his gaze didn't break from Mariah. "Please promise me that you'll never attempt a hike like this unless you've put at least twenty miles on a pair of shoes first," he said, carefully slipping the first shoe onto Scotty's foot.

"What?" asked Scotty with glazed-over eyes. He set his shoed foot on the ground and extended out his other foot for Levi to slip the remaining sock and shoe on.

"Forget it," said Levi with a grunt. "You won't remember any of this."

"You're better than I thought," said Mike, adjusting the belt at his waist. "This kid wouldn't even let me take off his boots. You're a miracle worker."

"This is all her," Levi said, pointing to Mariah. "If you don't believe me, stare into her eyes for a minute and try not to become a complete babbling idiot."

Mike humphed out his disbelief. "I've met some real charmers, but no woman can take away pain like that." He worked his way over to sit on the other side of Mariah on the picnic bench.

When Levi stood after finishing with Scotty's feet, Mariah turned to Mike and said, "Thanks for breakfast. It was delicious."

Scotty left as quietly as he'd come, but this time with a dopey smile on his face.

Mike tilted his head to the side and stared into Mariah's face but didn't speak.

She glanced over at Levi and mouthed, "What's wrong with him?"

Levi chuckled as he downed his breakfast in five bites. The salty, high carb and protein mixture was the perfect way to prepare for their hike. "Time for us to hit the trail." He clipped Mariah's backpack to his, then threw them both onto his back.

"Hold up a minute." Mike walked to his vehicle for a minute and returned with a knee brace for Mariah. He still held a facial expression of shock as he handed it to her.

Levi gave him an "I told you so" look and shook Mike's hand, palming him a hundred-dollar bill. "Thanks for everything, man."

Once on the trail, Levi watched Mariah carefully to see how badly she limped. She favored her right leg, but her limp had dissipated almost entirely. "How's the brace working?"

"Great. My knee feels more stable."

"Good. Did you take any pain medication this morning?"

"Do six ibuprofens count?"

"What!"

"Kidding," she said with a playful smile. "I took three Advil and one Tylenol. Mike told me that it works best to take them together."

"I'm surprised Mike was able to say anything with how you had him in a voodoo trance."

"Voodoo trance?" she said, picking up a stick from the trail and throwing it into the river. "What's that?"

"Witchery. You bewitch men."

"Oh, is that all? I thought you meant that I torture them with my dark sorcery."

He looked at her sideways. "Do you?"

"You tell me," she said with a wink.

"Yes. Absolutely. One hundred percent. Now let's talk about dreams."

She ignored his request. "What *I* want to know is if you really tipped the forest ranger a hundred-dollar bill for bringing us breakfast?"

He'd tried to be more discreet with his gift to Mike. "I guess you could see it as a tip. Career rangers in national parks like this one can make a sweet penny, upwards of a hundred-thousand-dollar salary, but not the less experienced, seasonal rangers like Mike. They're basically making minimal wage but they do it because they love helping people and living in nature, like wildland firefighters."

"You're a good man, Levi Grant. You must've been raised right."

"I could say the same for you. I like what your mom told you about the rain on a sunshiny day. She sounds like a really wonderful lady."

"She is. So's my dad. I haven't seen them for a while, but they're everything to me. Wait," she said, stopping to lean against a large boulder. "Did you say sunshiny?"

He rubbed his sweaty palms into his pants. "Mariah, I need to tell you something."

"About being a smokejumper? You read my mind. Are you trying to tell me that you don't do it for the paycheck? That you do it because you love it?" She bit her bottom lip and stared off into the river. "I hope this doesn't come off wrong.

I'm not trying to dis your choice in careers, but have you thought about how long you'll be a smokejumper?" There was pain in her eyes, like what he'd seen in them last night when she'd kissed him.

"Being a wildland firefighter is for the young. I'm pushing it, being almost thirty. Luckily, there's a waiting list to become a smokejumper. I'll need to let someone else have a turn someday. Otherwise, I think I might do it forever."

Her face lifted into a hopeful expression. She did a little hop, then started walking again. "Is there anything that might make you think about changing careers?"

He took a moment to choose his words carefully. Considering her many career related comments, she didn't care for him being an attorney, or a shoe salesman, or a smokejumper. He was starting to wonder if anything would impress her. "I'm guessing I'll adjust my life's goals someday. That would depend on who I'm setting my goals *with*." She glanced back at him with a shy smile but didn't speak. He took a leap of faith. "I have this idea of setting my goals in October instead of January. Does that sound crazy to you?"

"It's only crazy if you say it out loud."

He grabbed her hand. "And what if I *shout* it out loud?"

Her eyes danced. "Then you'd be certifiable."

A high-pitched scream echoed down the canyon.

"Fire!" someone yelled. "Help!"

Levi's eyes went wide. "I have to go," he said, barreling past her.

"Wait, Levi! Don't leave..." Her voice trailed off in to a whisper, her hopes disappearing along with him as he ran out of sight.

CHAPTER TEN

"*I*t's happening," Mariah whispered to herself, biting the last of her nails off as an emptiness settled into her core. She didn't have it in her to compete with Levi's love for firefighting. And from the looks of it, it wouldn't matter if she even tried. He would go when called, and leave her without a second's thought."

When her pounding heart finally calmed enough to get her bearings, she started along the trail again. Her knee felt a hundred times better than yesterday, but it still ached every time she lifted it. She glanced in the direction Levi had disappeared. She could walk at an okay pace, but there was no way she could run after Levi without collapsing. She had to have faith that Levi knew what he was doing, and that he would be okay.

She was on her own. Again.

"Hiking alone?"

She turned to see a group of middle-aged men on horseback, approaching her from behind.

"That depends," she said, plastering on a friendly smile.

One of the men climbed off his horse and began walking

toward her. The scene was right out of a humorous western movie; the kind where city slickers spend a weekend on a ranch. The cowboy who'd stepped off his horse and came to her side was the only man in the group who looked comfortable in his cowboy boots and Wrangler jeans. "My horse is tired of me," he said, patting his horse. "I'm too fat for him and you look like you could use a ride."

"I couldn't take your horse," she said in protest. She'd simply meant that she wouldn't mind some company for a while because she was freaked out that Levi had sprinted towards his death.

"Nonsense. I spent all day on this guy yesterday and I need to stretch my legs today. I insist," he said, holding the reins out to her.

"On one condition," she said, placing her right foot in the stirrup and pushing herself up onto the horse. "That you won't hesitate to tell me when it's time for me to get off this beautiful animal."

He placed his hand to his chest over his heart. "I'm Henry and you have my word."

"Mariah." She felt a twinge of guilt. She'd told Levi that she wanted to finish the hike by walking the entirety of the trail. She hadn't lied when she'd said it, but her determination had also been the result of her pride. She'd been on a course to prove Sebastian wrong, but she didn't feel that same way anymore. Somehow, with Levi, she didn't need to prove anything to anyone, even herself. She felt comfortable in her own skin. She stared down at her thick thighs, but they didn't seem as thick today as they did yesterday.

Henry pointed up the trail at the horse in front of them. "We're here to celebrate my buddy's fiftieth birthday. You must have a good reason to be here, hiking the Grand Canyon alone."

"It was my New Year's resolution to get fit. And I guess to celebrate my birthday as well."

"Birthday!" he shouted to his friends.

They all cheered.

She held up a finger. "Do you think it's cheating if I'm riding a horse when I'd set the goal to get into shape?"

"That depends on your *ultimate* goal," he said, stroking his horse's mane.

She glanced down at her stomach. "To lose weight."

He nodded. "I understand. But you need to ask yourself why. Are you doing it to curb your risk of diabetes or other diseases? To have more energy and feel better? Or are your goals based purely on body image?"

"Are you a therapist?" she asked with a teasing smile as her body swayed from side to side, following the horse's motions.

"You're sharp. I have a PhD in equine-assisted psychotherapy. But don't let the title scare you."

"Can I ask you something?"

"Shoot."

"You said it looked like I could use a ride. Why?"

He wiped sweat from his forehead and took in a deep breath. "Mostly because of the worry on your face. You were hiking alone but I'm guessing that wasn't always the case. Your left knee is braced and you aren't carrying any water."

"My backpack!" she exclaimed, feeling her back. "He ran off with it."

"There's the anxious expression I saw earlier. What happened?"

"It's not what *happened*. It's what I *fear* will happen." She looked up at the clear, light blue sky, the same color as Levi's eyes. "Maybe I do need a psychotherapist." Whoever said God works in mysterious ways was wrong. At least when it concerned her, God worked in plain sight, in simple, straightforward ways.

"And what do you fear?" Henry asked in a slow, gentle voice.

"I have a friend who's a wildland firefighter." Her voice caught in her throat. She swallowed. "He ran off about an hour ago when we heard someone yell fire."

"Mariah, I'm sorry to tell you this, but you don't need a psychotherapist. Your anxiety is normal and warranted." His attention shot up the sides of the trail. "I don't see any smoke. Do you?"

Mariah looked up and down the canyon. "No."

"What do you think the probability is that your friend is in danger?"

There couldn't be a raging fire without smoke, but her dream had been so vivid—especially the part where her kiss woke him from a death sleep. She touched her fingertips to her lips, reliving the kiss. "Next to none, I'm guessing."

"Your fear, although warranted, can be talked through. How do you feel now, after having discussed it?"

She shrugged. "Calmer. So, you don't think I suffer from abandonment issues?"

His brows knit together. "Did a therapist tell you that?"

She scratched her chin, trying to decide if she should tell him. "Ex-boyfriend."

"Ha!" he yelled, throwing his head back. "Those closest to us...or those *wanting* to be closest to us, sometimes use manipulative, hurtful tactics they don't even realize they're using."

"As much as I told myself, and him, he was wrong, I started to believe him."

"Therein lies the danger. When you were dating him, did you feel beautiful, or like you could never measure up to his expectations?"

"When you put it like that…" Her voice faded as a dark cloud of shame hung over her head with the thought that she'd allowed Sebastian to make her feel inferior.

"It's time to celebrate," Henry said with increased zeal.

"My birthday?" Mariah asked.

"That's one reason. Why else should we celebrate?"

"Would another reason be that I broke up with Sebastian. That I've grown stronger and more mature through my experiences with him?"

He rubbed his palms together. "See, you've proven my point."

"What's that?"

"That you simply need to talk through what's on your mind. You'll come up with your own solutions. You're smart and kind. Never allow anyone to make you feel otherwise."

"Thanks, Henry. I should pay you for the horseback ride and therapy session."

"I take checks, Venmo, and all major credit cards," he said with a hearty laugh.

Her friendly conversation with Henry, which could've been classified as a psychotherapy session, continued for the next three hours. She didn't see any sign of Levi along the way, but nor did she see any smoke. She'd hoped they would run into each other at some point on the trek. She'd woken up that morning in such a good mood, knowing she'd be spending at least one day with him before they separated and returned to their own lives. How could she miss someone so much when she hadn't spent any substantial time with him? Especially considering he'd left her on the trail alone. It didn't make sense, and yet she felt the void of not having him next to her.

The horses came to a halt. "This is where we part," said Henry. "We need to rest and water the horses, then we're looping back down to Phantom Ranch."

"I can't thank you enough," said Mariah, dismounting from the horse. Her left knee ached, but her legs are what killed her, particularly her thigh muscles; they screamed with every step. Luckily, the pain lessened as she walked in a circle around Henry's horse. The key was to keep moving, not stop or sit. Levi had been right when he'd said she'd have sore legs after yesterday's hike. If Henry and his gang hadn't come along, she didn't know how she would've survived walking the ten miles, let alone without water or electrolytes. She glanced up the trail. "Do you know how much farther it is to the top?"

"About a mile and a half," Henry said with a wide grin. "You got this, Mariah." He pulled a leather water canteen with a long strap from his saddle's pouch and looped it over her head so it hung across her body. Each of the five men had their own rustic leather canteens, which resembled something out of a historical trading outpost's gift shop, but they drank from disposable water bottles.

"I can't take this from you, Henry."

"It's a gift, Mariah. To remember us by. And you need it to stay hydrated."

"Photo!" she shouted, turning around and pulling her phone from her pocket. "My phone has one percent battery life left. Let's hurry." She held out her arm and took several selfies with the guys next to their horses. From that angle, her head looked ten times bigger than theirs, but that was okay. She wasn't planning on entering a beauty contest today. She looked like she'd tumbled down the Grand Canyon, and she smelled like she belonged in the corral with the horses.

Mind over body, she repeated over and over to herself as she climbed the last leg of her journey. Where others stopped to take photos, she focused straight ahead. She seldom glanced to her sides, even at her fellow, tired travelers. She took comfort in the fact that she didn't look much more haggard than the rest of them.

An hour into her last push, a handful of senior women grouped around her on the thin trail. Their silver hair glowed in the mid-day sun. She loved to see their endurance and spunk as they joked with each other, discussing how they'd hiked the Grand Canyon one more time without dying.

"Congratulations!" said Mariah to the more talkative woman of the group. There was always one gregarious leader. "You're inspiring. I say this with complete sincerity. I hope to have the same lively initiative someday as you ladies. I came here to prove something to myself, but I'm now realizing that it was more to prove myself to someone else."

"There's nothing wrong with that," their spunky leader said with resolve. "My goal was to finish this hike without trekking poles, so these are for you," she said, handing Mariah her poles. She looked Mariah up and down in a way that only grandmothers could do without being offensive. "Don't take this the wrong way, but you need my trekking poles more than I do."

Mariah laughed. "You're right. I could use poles. I lost mine." She thought about how her poles were inside of her backpack that Levi carried...somewhere. "That doesn't matter now. But I'll be fine. I don't want to take your poles from you."

"You're not taking them from me. They're already yours. Someday you'll come across someone who needs them more than you do, and they'll find a new home. Until then, may they make your journey lighter."

"Thank you," said Mariah, allowing the poles to take the pressure off her knees. "Can I get a photo with you wonderful ladies?" They stopped long enough to snap a photo, then the fit women were on their way again, blasting up the trail.

If they can do this, you can too, Mariah. Kick it into gear! she told herself with renewed purpose. A moment later, her phone rang. "I have reception!" she said with glee, answering the call from Sebastian. "Sebastian?" she said.

"Mariah." He said her name, then her phone died. She looked at her phone and laughed. "That about sums up this adventure." She pocketed her phone and kept moving. If she stopped, she may not ever start up again. Her thigh-burn was unlike any other pain she'd ever experienced, which was a blessing, because it drew her mind away from her knee injury and the possibility that she would need surgery.

"Mariah!" Sebastian's voice rang loud and clear.

She palmed her dead phone. "I'm hearing voices. This isn't good."

"Mariah," Sebastian said again, but this time the sound came from the top of the trail. He was waving for her to come to him. She felt like a toddler, being encouraged to take her first steps by an overeager caregiver. She wanted to laugh but didn't have the energy. All she wanted was a cleansing shower, or better yet, a long, hot bath.

The last few steps weren't what she's anticipated. She'd imagined the end being similar to the finish line of a race where she'd get a second wind to run through the yellow tape. There wasn't any tape, only her ex-boyfriend with a cheesy smile on his face. Her feet felt like lead and her body begged for food and rest. She mustered a smile when she reached the top and Sebastian embraced her. At least he smelled good.

"I was so worried about you. Levi called his brother a few minutes ago and said that you'd been separated early into the hike today."

"Separated?" she said with distain. "Is that how he put it?"

She was in no humor for Levi's excuses. He'd left her. Plain and simple.

"Come with me," Sebastian said, ignoring her dark mood. He pulled her to an overlook.

Her hand flew to her mouth. "I did that?" she exclaimed as she stared out at the deep, grand expanse. Tears pooled in her eyes. She hadn't hiked the full length of the canyon, but she'd hiked a huge portion of it. "I hiked *that*...with an injured leg?" While hiking, she'd kept her focus straight ahead, concentrating singularly on her goal to reach the top, not stopping to see what she was surmounting along the way. "I had no idea I was hiking that." She pressed a hand to her chest, allowing her tears to flow freely as she stared out across the canyon.

Out of the corner of her eye, she saw Sebastian drop to one knee. Her jaw slacked. She had to stop him, but it was too late.

He took hold of her left hand while her right hand still pressed against her chest. "Mariah, will you marry me?"

"Mariah." Her father's voice echoed. She looked up to see both her parents, and Sebastian's. She wanted to run and embrace her parents, but she needed to deal with Sebastian first. She smiled at her dad. He returned her smile with a thumbs up, his signature gesture for her.

Her hand went heavy. She looked down to find a diamond ring adorning her finger.

~

"She's at the top?" Levi shouted into his phone as he set off at a sprint up the hill. "How's that possible? I've been running up and down the trail, asking every single person if they've seen her. She would've had to run the entire way to make it up in that time. And there's no way that was physically possible."

"Levi," said Andy in a heavy voice. "You'll want to get up here quick."

Panic struck, causing his adrenaline to spike. "Why? What's wrong? Did mountain rescue haul her out?" That would've been the only explanation for her reaching the top that quickly. "Is she hurt?" he panted out.

"It's not that. Head to the lookout when you get here."

"Tell me already," Levi begged, reaching the end of the trail, then tearing through the crowd of people who waited for their chance to capture the perfect overlook photo. He skidded to a stop when he caught sight of Mariah.

Her entire face lit with a full smile while happy tears flowed down her cheeks. Sebastian was down on one knee beneath her. And on her finger rested a diamond ring.

Andy came to Levi's side and put his arm around his shoulder. "You should've seen the production Sebastian put on last night. He was up here for hours, waiting to propose to her. When I got here, he had battery operated light strings hung everywhere. He must've paid off a ranger for that. Man, he was upset when I told him that Mariah was camping with you and you were hiking out with her. What happened? Why did she come out a few minutes before you?"

Levi's arms went slack at his sides. "Why does she look so happy?"

Andy shrugged. "Don't women usually look happy when they get engaged?"

"She *wants* to marry him? I don't understand." *She kissed me!* But she'd never explained her dream to him. Maybe she'd been kissing Sebastian in her dream. But she'd broken up with him. Levi rubbed his fingers deep into his temples. He had to talk to her. Ask her why she would agree to marry a man she didn't love. "I have to know," he said, stepping through the circle of onlookers that surrounded Sebastian and Mariah.

Mariah's eyes lifted and locked with Levi's. She stumbled back toward the edge. He lunged forward, grabbed hold of her, and pulled her to the ground on top of him, preventing her from tumbling over the railing to an insanely steep drop and sure death.

"What are you doing?" she asked in an angry tone.

"Saving you. You're welcome."

"From what?" she asked defiantly, but she made no attempt to get off him.

He pointed to the cliff's edge.

Her eyes went wide as she looked down the side of the cliff. "I was that close to falling over?"

"You can't marry that guy."

Her eyes narrowed. "Give me one good reason why I shouldn't marry him."

He moistened his lips and swallowed, staring at her mouth. "You asked me to stay."

"You're right. I did. But you *still* left the tent and then you left me again this morning to fend for myself today without any water or hiking poles."

"I thought people were in danger but it was a small camp stove fire. They had it out before I reached them. I came back ten minutes later, and you'd disappeared. I've been running up and down this insane canyon trying to find you all morning."

Her eyes softened. "You've been looking for me?"

He ran his fingers along her neck. "Tell me you need me. Kiss me again," he begged her.

"What?" she said, her face registering surprise.

"Can I remind you?" he said, holding the back of her neck while he reached up to kiss her.

Before their lips met, Sebastian pulled her off him. "It

looks like you're stuck. Let me help you."

Before Levi could protest Sebastian's intervention, Andy yanked Levi up by his arm. "Levi, the car's waiting to take us to the helicopter. We've gotta go now, or we'll miss our ride. I need to be back in Vegas in less than two hours to meet with my crew."

Levi reached for Mariah but Andy pulled him away. "Ask me, Mariah," he begged her as she embraced a man he guessed was her father. "Ask me not to leave you." Mariah stared at him but didn't speak. "Please don't marry him, Mariah."

They were in the back of a car and pulling away with Mariah's name still on his lips.

"Let her go, Levi," Andy said, handing him a bottle of vitamin water. "Drink this. You haven't followed your own advice, have you?"

"What?" Levi asked in a daze.

"You're dehydrated," he said with a shake of his head. "I'm calling my doctor. He's going to put an IV in your arm the moment we land."

Levi rested his head back against the headrest and closed his eyes, hating himself for allowing Andy to drag him away from Mariah, but at least she was safe...in Sebastian's arms. He pounded his fists into his seat.

I failed.

CHAPTER ELEVEN

The moment Levi drove away, Mariah said goodbye to Sebastian forever. He fell silent and pouted, but his parents were there to comfort him.

Her heart tore to pieces, knowing she hadn't responded to Levi when he'd asked her to ask him to stay. Is that how it went down? Her head spun. She'd been in a state of shock from Sebastian's proposal and her parents' presence, not to mention how Levi repeated things she'd said to him in her dream. Had she really kissed him? She'd become so flustered that she hadn't been able to speak, and then Levi was gone.

Her dad had a blanket and an overnight bag ready for her in the back seat of his Ford truck. He'd known she would reject Sebastian's proposal, and yet he still came, or maybe that's why he'd driven two days—to bring Mariah home.

"Thanks for coming to get me," she said with a yawn, climbing into the back seat of her father's truck, taking care to not jostle her knee too much in the process.

Her mom asked her a question, but the words floated in the air, never quite making it down to her ears before she fell asleep. She woke six hours later when they pulled into the parking lot of a motel.

"I can't believe I'm so tired after a three-hour horseback ride."

"Really?" said her dad with a laugh. "That's what you're calling the last few days? A three-hour horseback ride?"

Mariah stretched her back. "When you put it that way..." She caught the scent of her stench. "How have you two seriously put up with my smell all afternoon?"

Her mother looked back at her and smiled. "Nose plugs."

"Ha ha," said Mariah with a roll of her eyes while she giggled in her throat.

"We stopped and bought a few ice packs," her mom said, pointing to the pads on Mariah's knee. "Andy said you most likely tore your ACL. Your father has already spoken to the orthopedic surgeon in town. You have an appointment set for next week. He said the swelling needs to go down before they can do anything."

"You talked to Andy?" Mariah stuttered out.

"He's a very nice young man," her mother said with a look of interest.

Her dad tapped his steering wheel. "He asked us to join him for dinner last night, and then again for breakfast this morning. He wanted to make sure that we knew you were in good hands with Levi, but you didn't seem too keen on the boy when you first saw him at the top."

"Misunderstanding," she said, staring out the window while her father parked. "He's an incredible person. One of the best men I've ever met."

"That's all I needed to know," her father said with a clap of his hands. A hint of a smile played at his lips.

"What does that mean?" Mariah asked with a wrinkle of her brow.

"It means we're stopping in Sun Valley on our way home."

"What? Seriously? Look at me," Mariah said, staring down at her dirt-encrusted pants and socks. "I'm an absolute mess."

"We brought a few of your favorite outfits."

"From a year ago. I'll never fit into those now."

Her dad cleared his throat. "It sounds like you're coming up with excuses to not see one of the best men you've ever met. Who happens to be attractive, kind, and rich."

"Rich?" she said with a dismissive flick of her wrist. "What are you talking about? He's a wildland firefighter and owns a small shoe store. The rent in that place is probably more than he gets in revenue."

Her parents looked at each other and laughed.

"What am I missing here?"

"Google him, darling," her mother instructed. "That's the first thing we did when we found out you were in Levi's care overnight." She coughed. "In his tent. If you want to scare your mother senseless, now you know how. Andy put us in touch with their mother. She's a very sweet woman who calmed my nerves."

"You spoke with Levi's mother?" Mariah covered her face from embarrassment as her father opened the door for her and helped her out.

Dad laughed. "It was that, or me hiking down to the ranch and yelling your name, waking the entire camp up until I found you."

Her mom linked her arm through Mariah's while they walked along the sidewalk to their room's exterior door. "Did you know that she's been in Africa on a safari? She invited us to come visit them in Sun Valley." She tapped her teeth. "Although, I don't think they'll be home from Africa by tomorrow."

"You called her in Africa while she was on a safari?" This was getting worse by the minute. "I'm almost thirty, Mom. She must think we're crazy."

They went inside and her mom stepped into the bathroom and kneeled next to the tub, splashing water around to rinse it out.

"Actually, she really wants to meet you. Like really really wants to meet you. Levi must've told her about you." She dumped a box of Epson salts into the tub and held her hand over the water, checking the temperature.

"Thanks for starting my bath," Mariah said, shooing her parents out of the bathroom, then stripping her clothes off. She glanced at the toilet and wondered when she'd gone to the bathroom last. "Well, that's scary," she said to herself as she slowly lowered herself down into the scalding water. She released a sigh of relief as her muscles tensed, then relaxed. "Levi, rich? No way," she said, digging her phone out of her pant's pocket. It wasn't there. "Hey, Mom!" she called out. "Could you bring me my—"

"Phone," her mom said, looking to the side as she entered the bathroom. She leaned down to hand Mariah her phone.

"Why is Levi's photo already up on my screen?" Mariah asked as her mom dipped out of the room.

Lead counsel for the Grant Family Holdings to appear in court on Monday, read the first article. *The Grant Family Foundation donates millions toward cancer research,* the second article was titled. *Billionaire Grant Brothers named most eligible bachelors.* Her heart sunk. She relaxed her arm, dropping the phone to the floor next to the tub with a clunk. Didn't every girl dream of marrying a rich man? She couldn't pinpoint why it bothered her that Levi was rich. Was it because he hadn't told her? Or because she was no longer in his league? With that kind of money, he could date models and movie stars. She leaned her head back against the plastic tub surround and sighed.

What better place to have a pity party than in a tub? She let the tears flow. Twenty-eight years old with no job, no money, with a chubby, sore and miserable body that needed expensive surgery, no boyfriend and no prospects. The only thing she needed to ask herself was how long she could stay in the tub, thus avoiding her parent's inquisitive smiles. If only she hadn't told them how much she adored Levi.

$\sim$

The next day, Mariah stood outside Levi's shoe store, shivering. Her parents had brought her favorite red pleated skirt and white blouse. Unfortunately, the blouse was two sizes too small and her breasts were bubbling out. According to her mom, sometimes it was okay to show a little cleavage if it was only meant for a future husband. But Mariah wasn't there to catch or entrap Levi. She was there to say goodbye. She owed him that.

She waved goodbye to her parents as they drove down the street toward the Mandolin. Ever since Mariah raved about the Mandolin's French onion soup, her mother just had to try it.

At least Mariah would have a few minutes alone with Levi. Her parents had left her on the curb with smiles on their faces, believing she was there to express her undying love to him. They were in for a surprise.

With a deep inhale, she stepped into the store. "Levi?" she called, walking to the checkout desk while she searched the store with her eyes.

Voices originated from the storage room. A middle-aged woman stepped out of the room. Mariah glanced down at her overflowing bosom and jumped behind a rack of winter scarves. She pulled one off the rack and wrapped it around her neck, allowing it to flow down, ultimately covering her chest.

"What happened?" the woman asked Levi. "I thought you

were going to get her to fall in love with you? You're losing your touch, Levi. First, I'm going to call Annie. You need help. And second, I'm going to call that private detective."

"You've already spoken to her parents, Mom. Why would you need a private detective? Mariah is going to need time to process this," Levi argued. "You can't just tell her we've found her biological family and expect her to be grateful."

Mariah bit the inside of her mouth, causing warm, metallic blood to fill her mouth. Her arms and legs quivered. "You what?" she said in a breathy voice.

"Mariah!" he exclaimed, running towards her.

She backed up when he reached for her. "You followed me to the Grand Canyon to make me fall in love with you? And you know...you know my mom? That's..." she stuttered out. "That's not possible." She placed a hand to her forehead to stay her dizziness and told her stomach to quit churning. "I talked to the adoption agency. You can't know my biological mom."

"Mariah." Levi's mom touched Mariah's hand gently. Her countenance had altered from a disapproving, grumpy mother to a sensitive steward.

Mariah didn't know what to think or feel. Levi and his mother were sensitive one minute, then dismissive the next.

"I'm sorry," his mother said. "That came off as brusque. I've been traveling for two days and we've been so worried about you for so long. Please let me explain."

"I need air," Mariah said, stumbling to the door. "I can't breathe. Please, don't follow me, Levi. I need time. You understand that, right? You understand how I need time to process this?"

"I do," Levi said with a nod, remaining completely still as his concerned eyes danced around her face.

Mariah leaned against the doorframe before stepping out

into the cold. "And for the record, I did fall in love with you. So, let's just add heartache to heartache."

"How can you let her go?" Levi's mom whined as the door slowly shut.

Mariah hobbled toward the epitome of comfort, her daddy's strong arms. By the time she'd reached the Mandolin, her entire body was laden with goose bumps. If she'd had one more layer on, then she would've been fine. The scarf she'd taken from Levi's store hadn't kept her warm, but at least it covered her chest so she wouldn't feel uncomfortable walking into the fine dining establishment. She gave her eyes a minute to adjust to the low light before she searched out her parents.

The receptionist caught Mariah's eye. "I believe your party is sitting at table twenty-eight. If you'll follow me, I'll take you to them."

"Twenty-eight?" Mariah repeated.

Her daddy walked up and wrapped his bear arms around her. "Want to talk about it?"

She buried her face in his chest. "Not really. Can we just get a bowl of soup and drive home please? I need my bed."

He expelled a long breath but didn't answer her.

"Daddy?"

He cleared his throat. "Pumpkin, this is going to be an adjustment for all of us. I'm as scared as you are right now."

She lifted her face and stared into his misty, kind brown eyes. "I don't understand."

"Your mom and I walked in at the same time as a beautiful woman. Her face is unforgettable. We knew God had placed us together today for you, so we asked the woman if she wanted to sit with us. We've had a nice conversation for the past half hour."

"But why would you invite a beautiful woman—" Mariah's voice broke when she saw the woman sitting with her mother in the nearest booth to the kitchen. Unfamiliar, conflicting emotions of anger and hurt blended with peace and love in her breast in a jarring, painful way. "I can't do this, Daddy," she said through tears. "I'm not ready."

"Yes, you are. You've been ready for this meeting for a long, long time. She's a good woman who loves you as much as we do. That doesn't seem possible, but I see it in her eyes...your eyes. Go see," he said with encouragement.

Mariah swallowed down her fear as she slowly stepped to the booth. Her mom jumped up, hugged her, then motioned for her to sit across from the woman.

The woman rested her folded hands on the table. "Thank you for meeting with me, Mariah. Do you have any questions for me?"

"No. I have around two million."

The woman giggled in her throat, causing Mariah to sniff back her tears.

"Are you my mother?"

"No. I'm your mother's sister, Charlotte Terrence. Your mom passed away in a plane crash when you were young. And your father passed away serving our country in Iraq before you were born. He was a hero."

"Do you know why she put me up for adoption?"

Charlotte stared down at her hands. "It was my fault. I'm so sorry, Mariah. When your mom told me that she wanted to marry your father after only knowing him a month, I told her that she was being impulsive and reckless. I begged her to break up with him." She wrung her hands. "They got engaged. And the day he shipped out overseas, she stopped talking to me. When I finally tracked her down eight months later, she'd already given you up for adoption." She stared into Mariah's eyes. "She fell into a deep depression when your father died. I wish I knew what she was going through. I didn't know she was pregnant. I wish I'd reached out to her sooner. She didn't feel like she could come to me and she thought you would have a better chance at happiness with a kind, happy couple." She looked over at Mariah's parents. "She chose well."

Mariah folded her hands over Charlotte's. "Thank you. It helps to understand the circumstances."

"Mariah, I want you to know that your mother thought about you and prayed for you every day."

Mariah's heart warmed. "Was she happy?"

Charlotte nodded. "You sound just like her. She put the happiness of others before her own. But yes. She was happy. It took her a while to become herself again, but she pulled out of her depression to lead a joyful life. She had regrets. We all do, but she learned to be happy."

"I like that. How she *learned* to be happy. I think sometimes we just think that happiness should come naturally."

"Mariah, I want you to know that I'm here for you. You're as much family to me as are my own children." Her face lifted into a huge smile. "And your cousins can't wait to meet you, but we can take this as slow as you'd like." She glanced toward the waiting area. "And your parents are now family as well and invited to all family gatherings with us and with the Grants."

"The Grants are family?" Mariah asked with wide eyes.

"Not blood related," she said with a wink. "Although we've wanted to unite our families in blood for years. So, if *any* of the Grant boys catch your eye…"

"Is it that obvious?" It felt so easy and safe talking to her.

"Your mother was my baby sister. I knew by the expression on her face every time she fell in love, but she only had that same look in her eye once, when she told me about your father."

"But Levi and I come from different worlds. He grew up

rich and privileged. I'll never fit into that world. I'll never be rich."

Charlotte twisted her lips. "You are now. Whether you want to be or not. You're my heir. I placed you in my trust when I found out about your birth. We just needed to find you. I've been searching for you since you turned eighteen."

Mariah didn't even attempt to stop the tears from coming because she knew it would be futile. "You've been searching for me for ten years?"

"And now you see why we left our African safari and jumped on a plane the minute we heard you'd been found. And it was all thanks to Levi."

"Levi? How?"

"When he noticed you in his shoe store."

"Actually," she said, pointing a finger at the ceiling. "That was all me. I wrecked my bike and Levi came sprinting out of his store to help me. If I'd never hit the pavement, we wouldn't be here talking."

"That sounds like your mom. The only time she wasn't clumsy was when she was in the ocean."

"I love the ocean."

"It's in your blood. Our ancestors came from the Faroe Islands, halfway between Norway and Iceland. We've always lived by the sea. Our people were some of the first settlers in St. Augustine, Florida in the 1400s, and then in San Francisco during the gold rush, and now in Costa Rica. And we sail."

"Sail?" Mariah exclaimed with excitement.

"But we have time to discuss all of that. I think someone really wants to talk to you," she said, motioning to the bar.

Levi sat with his back to them but glanced over as if he wanted to be a part of the conversation, yet he kept his distance to give them space.

"Are you sure that I fit with Levi? Look at him. He's

gorgeous, smart, and super wealthy. He could have any girl he wants."

"And what if he *wants* someone who's gorgeous and smart and super wealthy?" she said with a teasing smile. "What if he wants you?"

"He thinks I'm smart and gorgeous?"

"He'd be a complete idiot if he didn't. And Levi's no idiot."

Charlotte took hold of Mariah's hands. "And I won't tell you to wait if you want to marry him in a month."

"But I can't lose him like my your sister lost my biological dad. It would kill me. He's chosen a noble but dangerous career."

"I've decided to give someone else a chance to be a smokejumper," Levi said, standing next to the table. "And I was thinking a week, not a month."

Mariah's breath caught in her chest.

Charlotte stood, kissed Mariah on the forehead, and left gracefully.

Levi took one look at the bench that Charlotte vacated and shook his head. "Sitting across from you isn't going to work for me," he said, scooting in next to her on her bench. The candle lighting was just right to cast a soft glow over his face. "I promised you something last night."

"Hmm?" she hummed out, not trusting herself to speak.

"You gave me the best kiss of my life the other night."

Her hand flew to her mouth with the realization that she had indeed kissed him in the tent.

"Then I promised to protect you for as long as you would allow me to. You asked me to stay. Now I'm asking you to stay with me, Mariah. Stay with me here in Sun Valley or stay with me in Sacramento. I don't care where we are. But please don't leave me. I love you and never want to be apart from you again."

She reached up and touched his cheek. "Are you sure that's what you want?"

"More than anything in the world," he said, tilting her chin up and lowering his face until their lips met.

Glowing flames shot through her chest and radiated out her fingertips. "Then I guess I'm here to stay. And if I'm working at the running store, I won't have to steal scarves to cover up with."

"Please don't cover up," he said, removing the scarf from her neck. "Or I can't do this," he said, kissing her neck.

"Whoa there, cowboy," said Andy, standing at the front of the booth. "This is not that type of establishment. You'd think this was a French restaurant or something," he said with a wink. "Carry on, soldier. I'm bringing the two of you oysters and snails."

Mariah held up a hand to stop Andy, but lowered her hand when Levi kissed her fingers, causing her mind to blur. She didn't care what Andy brought them. As long as Levi held her in his arms, she was living her dream.

The End.

ABOUT THE AUTHOR

Raised in Milwaukee, Wisconsin and Atlanta, Georgia, Sarah currently calls the northern Utah mountains, and the southern Utah red rocks, home. She graduated in Human Development and spent several years working as a Human Resource Professional. Her human resource skills are now utilized managing a workforce of four young children. When Sarah's team is being trained off campus, she dedicates her time to writing inspirational stories.

She would love to hear from you and can be contacted at sarah@sarahgay.com. To register for new releases, promotions, and free recipes, sign up for her newsletter at sarahgay.com.

    amazon.com/author/sarahgay
    facebook.com/sarah.gay.125
    bookbub.com/authors/sarah-gay

www.ingramcontent.com/pod-product-compliance
Lightning Source LLC
Chambersburg PA
CBHW030352180626
46812CB00007B/2853